KILL DEPTH

STEVE METCALF

SEVEREDPRESS

KILL DEPTH

Copyright © 2024 by Steve Metcalf

WWW.SEVEREDPRESS.COM

ISBN: 978-1-923165-25-0

PROLOGUE
INTO THE ICE CHIMNEY

IT WAS ASTONISHING just how quickly a perfectly constructed plan could fall to shit. The submersible, N802 Galbreath, carried a crew of three on a straightforward search and rescue mission. Their goal was to locate a self-piloted exploratory drone that reported an error back to base an hour ago and then suddenly went offline. The control room was antsy because the drone represented an investment of several million dollars the military had made in Epsilon Complex. The ocean, unfortunately, didn't give a damn.

"Passing 10,000 feet, control," Samir said from the pilot's chair of the Galbreath.

"Copy that," came the response from the control room, nearly two miles above them. "Passing 10,000. That was the error depth, Galbreath."

"Copy that."

They slightly slowed their descent and all three men leaned closer to their respective bank of sensors. The Galbreath was one of the mid-size subs in the complex's fleet and was expressly designed for search, mapping and recovery. There were no frills built into the vessel's equipment load-out – which was why it was chosen for this mission. They had last received word from the drone at this depth and collectively hoped that its auto maneuvering protocols had kicked in before it bricked and sank to the bottom of the ocean. Management prayed to whatever they could think of that the Galbreath would find the expensive drone hovering blindly in the middle of the ice chimney … a few miles below the surface.

"Approaching 12,000," Samir said to both his crew and the control room.

"Copy that."

"We're coming up blank in the chimney, stick," Rodgers said from his position on the starboard side of the Galbreath.

"Hang on," the third man, Johnson, said from his position opposite Rodgers.

"What is it?" came a slightly distorted voice from the control room thousands of feet above them.

"I'm reading a," Johnson paused, adjusting some on-screen filters on his equipment. "I'm reading a horizontal void. Two hundred feet down, bearing zero six five." He looked up from the equipment with the readings locked in and hefted an eyebrow at the vessel's pilot, Samir. "It looks like a cave."

**

The Galbreath, the state-of-the-art rescue submersible, stood hovering near the western edge of the giant sinkhole the research vessels had been commissioned to explore. It was a "blue hole," almost a perfect circle, that had opened in the Antarctic Ocean. The hole itself sat on a relatively shallow continental shelf but it dropped a staggering depth into the Earth. They had so far sent AI-controlled drones to a depth of about 30,000 feet – nearly the depth of the Mariana Trench – but so far had not mapped the bottom. By contrast, the deepest Blue Hole that had been fully explored was the Dragon Hole in the South China Sea. It was just under 1,000 feet from the surface to the bottom.

The Antarctic Hole was carved nearly six miles into the Earth's crust. So far.

"Holding," Samir said over comms to the control room.

"Copy."

The Galbreath was hovering 12,000 feet into the chimney of the sinkhole facing a horizontal offshoot that could comfortably park a three-story building. It had appeared out of nowhere and it was massive.

"Whoa," Johnson said. He, Rodgers and Samir were all standing in the cabin of the submersible, leaning forward to stare out the curved front windows. The vessel rocked ever so slightly, and the three men looked at each other. The water in the chimney had generally been still but they seemed to be picking up some type of current from the horizontal shaft. The maneuvering propellers, however, did their job and kept the sub in position.

Ping.

Rodgers turned and took the two steps back to his bank of equipment.

"I'm getting a reading," he said over comms. "It looks like we're picking up the drone."

"Copy," the control room answered. "Distance?"

"It looks to be about 200 feet from the mouth of the cave," he said, leaning in toward one monitor in particular. "About 250 feet from our current position."

"Roger that," came the clipped voice from the control room thousands of feet above them. "Proceed and recover."

"Copy that, control," Samir said while he once again gripped the controls of the sub. The three men could hear the engine wind up and the vessel started moving forward into the mouth of the giant cavern.

Rodgers was tracking the drone's signal on his main screen and Johnson was mapping the features of the cave as they went. He reached up and wiped the sweat from his right temple – looked up and away from his monitor out the front of the Galbreath's cabin at the huge windows. The little sub had about a dozen lights on all around the vessel. They were powerful but were only barely scraping the edges of the cavern.

"Spooky," he said, blinking once and then looking back down at his instrument panel. "It's clearly a natural formation, but it's different than any other type of sea cave we've mapped."

"How so?" Samir asked over his left shoulder without moving his head.

"Well it's about ..." Johnson said and then was interrupted by a loud warning klaxon echoing throughout the sub.

"We're here," Rodgers said, looking up from his screen. "Fifty feet to starboard."

"Copy," Samir said and stopped the forward progress of the sub and started sliding to the right. The klaxon warning sirens continued blaring until Samir reached to the right side of his instrument panel and hit a button that left the warning lights blinking in the cabin but silenced the noise.

It didn't take long for the small sub to travel the fifty feet and pulled to a halt. Samir tilted the nose of the vessel down and began a slow spin to visually locate the missing, malfunctioning drone.

"Oh no," he said, finding it.

**

Mangled.

The self-propelled drone was roughly the size and shape of a riding lawnmower. It was bristling with a complex equipment array, however, made up of lights, cameras, sensors and antennas. This drone, however, looked like it had been run over by a tank. Half the big object was crushed, and the rest was covered in …

"Are those bite marks?" Samir said, leaning forward, squinting. He tried adjusting the angle of some of the mobile lights on the exterior of the Galbreath. "Are there sharks down here? Orcas?"

Rodgers had joined him at the front of the cabin. Johnson continued pushing his sensors forward as much as he could to get a better map of the cavern. He was able to "see" almost a quarter mile down the path – although the clarity of the images degraded significantly the farther away from the sub they got. It was almost like a video game from decades past. The monitor could draw distant objects with hardly any fine details, but the amount of features increased exponentially the closer to the actual equipment the images were. He had taken one look at the demolished drone and knew they wouldn't be staying for long.

"We should probably clamp it and examine it at the complex," he said to his crew, but mostly to himself.

Still leaning forward, Samir reached down to his instrument panel and activated the sub's claw arm and flipped on the maneuvering camera, similar to that of a car when it switched to reverse gear.

"Galbreath?" came a sharp retort from the control room. "Report?"

Samir was now piloting the sub forward until it was directly over top of the drone. He was watching the tiny screen intently, so Johnson responded.

"We've located the drone, control," he said. "It has sustained heavy damage. We're maneuvering to collect and return to base."

"Roger that."

Not only was there an audible clunk, muffled through the heavy water, but a slight lurch from underneath the sub as the huge metallic arms clamped around the corpse of the drone.

"At least the damn thing didn't sink to the center of the Earth," Samir said, a nervous laugh punctuating the sentence.

There was a soft whir as Samir retracted the heavy cables back up to the belly of the Galbreath to reduce drag as they piloted back to Epsilon Complex. Even though they had plenty of room to maneuver, he chose to tilt the nose of the craft up and reverse the 200 feet back to the mouth of the cave and the chimney of the sinkhole.

The lights kept blinking off and on signaling the warning klaxon even without the sound. It took them a few minutes to reach the entrance and Samir keyed his mic.

"Control," he said. "Drone is recovered. Heavy damage. We're in the pipe, heading back to base."

"Copy," came the voice from the control room 12,000 feet away. "Double-quick."

"Copy. Galbreath out."

Samir reached back to his instrument panel to switch the audible klaxons on to hopefully clear the warning. It only served to add sound to the blinking lights.

"Why are we still getting," he started but was interrupted by Johnson's sudden exclamation.

"Oh shit," he said, grabbing the armrests of his seat. "Incoming. Brace yourselves."

**

Crunch.

The Galbreath was thrown laterally and tumbled side over side into the center of the sinkhole chimney. The force had come out of the horizontal passageway and, as they had turned away from the entrance to begin their ascent, they had never registered a visual image. It was likely they had caught their attacker on one of the numerous cameras stationed around the outer hull of the sub, but they didn't have the time to check that now.

The self-stabilization protocols kicked in and righted the vessel but outside of the craft's correct orientation, everything was chaos.

Samir and Rodgers had managed to get strapped in before the impact, so they were going to have to deal with bruising and strained muscles. Johnson, however, wasn't as lucky. Had he reached for the four-point harness rather than the armrests, he might have been okay. As it was, he tumbled out of his chair and smashed his head against the bulkhead. He never lost consciousness, but a huge gash opened across his forehead nearly from temple to temple. It was bleeding profusely, and blood was splattering across the floor of the sub.

The initial warning klaxon was now joined by two other warnings – one signaling damage to the port engine bay and one signaling hull damage. Pipes had cracked along the interior of the sub – one leaking hydraulic fluid from the damaged propulsion system and the other had started spraying water.

Samir shook his head to try to clear it. He wiped the sweat from his face and dug it out of his eyes with the palms of both hands at the same time. Johnson stumbled back to his chair and slid into it, his face a blood veil. He tried to fasten his seatbelt, but his hands were slippery from the sweat and blood.

"Hull integrity 85% and falling," Samir said, reading the instrument panel. "Resetting engines and heading up to Epsilon. Do you have a fix?"

Rodgers was leaning in toward his own instrument panel and bank of monitors. Every few seconds he coughed ... and then winced in pain. He was certain that he had cracked a couple ribs when the force threw him against his harness. At least.

"Nothing clear, stick," he said. "Computer is having trouble registering a shape circling above us."

"Jesus Christ," Samir said with a sigh. "Control, do you copy? We were rammed by something that is now hovering between you and us. We're down an engine but are moving in your direction."

"Copy that, Galbreath," control said. The clarity of the audio had diminished significantly from their earlier transmissions. Samir worried that they had damaged the communications array as well as the pile of other broken equipment. "We can send depth charges to distract whatever attacked you."

"If you're going to do it, do it now," Samir responded. "We're passing 10,000 feet and I don't want you accidentally hitting us."

"Say again, Galbreath," control called back, in a clear panic. "You're breaking up."

"Shit," Samir said. "Send the depth charges *now*, control."

"Copy that. Sending depth charges."

Samir looked over at Johnson who kept trying to wipe the blood out of his eyes and man his station. He looked back over his other shoulder at Rodgers, who shook his head.

"It's still up there, Samir."

Samir nodded.

"Passing 10k. Hull integrity at 72%. I'm dumping all non-essential systems and putting them into engines. Maybe the depth charges and the looming presence of the complex might scare whatever it is away."

As he manipulated the system, most of the lights in the cabin went dark. Just as everything but the main lights outside shut off – the power diverted to propulsion. They now found themselves in near-darkness two miles below the surface of the Antarctic Ocean.

With a thump – almost a loving tap compared to the impact just minutes ago – the Galbreath jolted sideways and then continued on that path. They were moving laterally in the ice chimney and eventually smashed against the smooth wall of the sinkhole. With a sickening thud and then a horrific scraping sound, the port side of the sub was crunched and then dragged along the ocean wall as it still continued moving upward.

"Critical hull warning," Johnson called out. His face was painfully pale as the blood had slowed somewhat from the gaping head wound.

Suddenly, the remaining engine died as that side of the vessel was being destroyed against the frozen wall of the sinkhole. Yet another warning klaxon sounded –

this one related to propulsion. The small team heard a terrible crack as the hull was crunched inward and their momentum upward completely stopped. They were sinking.

"Burst transmit everything we collected," Samir called.

Rodgers began frantically punching keys on his console and then nothing. The small vessel was crushed inward like an empty soda can. It sank, lifelessly to the bottom of the pit ... dragging the nearly-rescued reconnaissance drone along behind it.

"Control," Samir tried. "Control, do you read us?"

There was a burst of static and then comms went completely dead. He looked at what was left of his instrument panel. Most of the controls were highlighted in black or red ... or completely dead. They had life support and about twenty percent of the total lights and cameras still operational around the exterior of the vessel.

Rodgers pulled the master switch and shut down all the warning signals – both sound and lights. They weren't going to make it back to the surface. Might as well not die with a headache.

"20,000 feet," Samir called over his right shoulder.

"Copy that," Rodgers said and looked over at Johnson. The man was strapped into his chair but had lost consciousness from a combination of the severe head trauma and the massive resulting blood loss.

"Johnson?" Samir called. There was no answer. Before he could call out again, he was distracted by a shape rushing past the bow windows of the sub. Both he and Rodgers had leaned forward in their chairs.

The object defied explanation: it was almost a visual trick. Nothing that big should be moving that fast.

Especially four miles deep in a chimney of ice water. They watched the enormous shadowy figure do a lazy figure eight in the distance, perfectly matching the descent of the sub. Suddenly, the monster turned and rushed directly toward them. All they could see was a gaping mouth filled with person-sized teeth exploding through the water.

Crunch.

The beast slammed directly into the front of the vessel, shattering the hull. The Galbreath imploded under the pressure of the Antarctic Ocean and sank lifelessly into the inky depths.

CHAPTER ONE
WELCOME TO EPSILON COMPLEX

THE UNITED STATES maintains three year-round research stations on Antarctica – Amundsen-Scott at the South Pole, Palmer on the peninsula and McMurdo Station on Ross Island. It was from the latter that the two men had left only an hour before. They had to take a circuitous route to avoid a nasty storm, but only needed to make it forty miles into the Ross Sea to get to the oceanic research center Epsilon Complex.

"You've heard of a sinkhole, right, sir?" the pilot called back into the passenger area over his headset microphone. They were flying along in a decommissioned and privatized Bell Super Huey, the UH-1Y Venom. It had been painted a deep royal blue with gold piping. Along its tail section and doors, now standing closed due to the extreme temperatures, was the highly stylized gold lettering for Allied Genetics … along with their corporate logo, a scorpion. The big helicopter thundered along, tearing the silent afternoon air to shreds.

"Sure," the passenger said. "Water eats away at the ground feet or miles down and the surface just caves in. A hole because the ground just sinks away."

"Scary as hell, sir," the pilot said with a chuckle. "The most publicized ones occur on land, swallowing a house, part of a road, bunch of cows. Whatever. But they happen in the oceans, too. Remember. The Earth is just over seventy percent covered in water. So, it makes sense."

"Yeah," the passenger said. "It makes sense."

"When they happen in the water, they're generally called a "blue hole" because the color changes. The water looks darker blue because the land has dropped away. Anyway, there are a couple big ones that people talk about. The Dragon Hole in the South China Sea is one. Dean's Blue Hole and the Great Blue Hole are both in the Caribbean. The Great Blue Hole is called that because it's so wide. Almost a thousand feet wide. But only about a third of that deep."

"Okay." The passenger paused. "That still seems pretty deep. More than 300 feet?"

The pilot continued without directly responding, banking gently to the south: "Most of the ones in the ocean were formed during ice ages when the sea level was lower and surface features got melted away by erosion. When the sea levels rose, they filled in these holes with water." He paused, letting all this sink in. "What we're looking at, though, is a true sinkhole. We have pretty detailed surveys of the Ross Sea and the Southern Ocean dating back decades. This," he said, smiling over his shoulder, "is new. As if miles of the seabed just sank away. We call it the Ice Chimney."

**

What started out as a strange little misshapen dot on the horizon slowly grew into a huge structure floating in the center of a giant blue circle in the ocean. The structure looked like a blend of a large oil drilling station and a futuristic research facility. Parts of the structure looked Spartan and purely functional while other sections were gleaming in their newness, polished to a violent sheen. There were also numerous observation decks with steel balconies backed by heavy-duty windows.

"Welcome to Epsilon Complex," the pilot said.

"That's quite a sight," the passenger said. "Who's in charge?"

"Onsite?" the pilot asked, but it wasn't really a question. "That would be Kelly Green. Her official title is Operations Manager, but she is the direct line to company management. She's running the show."

"Kelly Green," the man said, contemplatively.

"You know her, sir?"

The passenger shrugged and grinned.

"I used to," he said. "That's for damn sure."

The pilot nodded, swinging the big chopper around the north edge of the enormous platform, and lining up a landing on an octagonal section with a giant H stenciled on it in reflective thermoplastic paint. There were two other helicopters near the platform – clearly wheeled into their designated parking spots.

**

"Mr. Granville," said a man striding toward the Venom helicopter with his right hand outstretched and his left hand shielding his eyes from the diminishing wind from the huge blades. The passenger had stepped out of the seating area of the chopper while strapping a messenger bag across his chest and looping it around his back. He reached back into the Venom to grab what could have been a huge gym bag. It was black with a sports logo emblazoned along the side. It was stuffed to the hilt.

He turned to see the man and held out his own right hand.

"Tom, please," he said. "Or Thomas, if you prefer." He shook the man's hand.

"Great, Tom, I'm David Fontaine," the other man said and reached for Tom's travel bag. "I head the Section 3 research department. Allow me. We appreciate you making time and coming to visit us so quickly. If you'll follow me, I'll show you to your quarters. We have a debriefing at seventeen-hundred hours. Five o'clock. I'll try to get you squared away in the meantime."

Tom allowed himself to be led away from the helicopter as a ground crew scurried over to handle their post-flight checklist.

**

His quarters were a strange blend of a cruise ship room and a prison cell. It was about 200 square feet with no windows. Room for a full-size bed, a smallish loveseat and a little desk. The desk doubled as an eating area with a small microwave and dormitory fridge resting alongside. He had a toilet, sink and standing shower just off the entrance. Fontaine had put Tom's luggage on the foot of the bed and pulled out the small task chair that rested under the desk. He waved his hand to indicate that Tom should have a seat on the loveseat.

"The pilot gave you some sort of briefing, I assume," Fontaine said, smiling. He sat on the desk chair and somehow made it look comfortable. He had turned slightly to the side and slid his right arm out along the surface of the desk. "He likes to do that. Very proud of the complex."

Tom nodded.

"Yeah," he said. "The pilot talked about the sinkhole. The Ice Chimney. But he didn't talk about the facility much. Or the lost submersible. The reason I'm out here."

David Fontaine nodded, the grin never leaving his face. Tom was a consultant by trade with a long, distinguished resume. Military training, college education, advanced degrees. He had worked with numerous tech companies in the past on recovery, security or risk analysis assignments. His experience was a strange Venn Diagram with the two huge overlapping sections being hush-hush government contracts and projects for med-tech giant Allied Genetics. It was this overlap that prompted the call he received forty-eight hours ago. The Department of Defense and Allied Genetics were in bed together with Epsilon Complex and needed his objective experience to figure out what happened and how to correct it.

"You have the file," Fontaine said nodding toward the messenger bag. A thick report was sent by courier directly to Tom within hours of the dual-decision to bring him on. "Maybe I can help with what's not in the file. We'll have the briefing in a little bit, but you can take this time to ask me any questions you might have."

Tom unclasped the worn-leather messenger bag, now resting across his lap. He pulled out several thick manilla folders, a binder and a legal pad attached to a clipboard. He spread them all out along the thin coffee table that sat in between the love seat and the desk. Tom pulled open one folder and Fontaine could see that the reports were covered in notes, highlights and Post-its.

"Yeah," Tom said. "I've got some questions. But I kind of want to get into the stuff that's not in *here*."

Fontaine swallowed uneasily.

"Let's start with this facility," Tom said. "What the hell's going on here?"

**

"I'll spare you the boring details," Fontaine said. "Epsilon Complex is a two-stage deep-sea research facility. The top structure floats in a fixed position and is based on the superstructure of an oil drilling platform."

"I could see that coming in," Tom said. "How is it fixed? Clearly there's no way to drop anchor."

Fontaine nodded.

"Correct. There's absolutely no way a chained- or sea-anchor helps us in this situation. On each of the four legs of the platform there is affixed a massive propellor. They're tied to an AI weather system that is constantly reading currents, waves, air speed and about three dozen other factors. The propellors automatically change speed and direction, working together to keep the platform afloat and in a locked in position. In fact, there's a satellite in geosynchronous orbit …"

Tom cut him off.

"Is that stage two?" he asked. "The satellite?"

Fontaine shook his head.

"Tethered to the platform and hanging 200 feet down is the main observation deck," he smiled. "Invisible to prying eyes, the secondary platform is free to perform whatever experiments become necessary. There's a dive deck up above for submersibles and the secondary platform is tethered by not only a central pillar, but four express elevators to carry people, equipment and supplies back and forth."

"An underwater elevator," Tom said, shaking his head. "That doesn't sound the least bit safe."

Fontaine grinned.

"No, I imagine that it doesn't. They are connected via a steel mesh and vinyl-wrapped polymer. All proprietary. Very strong. Very safe. Been tested to hell and back the world over."

"I'll have to take your word for it."

Fontaine smiled, proud. Tom made some notes on a fresh piece of legal paper.

"How many drones are active?"

"There are none on mission right now," Fontaine said. "The remaining nine were recalled so regular maintenance could be performed until we got a fix on what happened in the chimney. We also have two remote controlled subs and six manned submersibles of various sizes and capabilities."

Tom nodded, making his notes. He didn't look up as he continued writing.

"How many successful drone missions were there before this?"

"Ten," Fontaine said. "The lost probe would have been the eleventh."

"None of them went to 12,000 feet? None of them reported a huge horizontal cavern in the side of the chimney?"

"No."

"Do you have any footage or recordings from the missing drone?"

"Yes."

"Do you have any footage or recordings from the missing sub? The Galbreath?"

"Yes."

Tom finally looked up. He put his pen down and sat up straight on the loveseat cushion.

"Is there anything you're not telling me?"

"Not at all," Fontaine said and paused. He sensed a lull in the conversation and rubbed the palms of both hands down the front of his pants. Tom smiled. He could place Fontaine geographically from it. It was a common, subconscious maneuver that nearly all Midwesterners made when it was getting to be time to end a conversation and leave. The move generally translated into something close to, *Whelp, I better let you go.*

Fontaine stood up from the small desk chair and nodded to Tom.

"As I said, there will be a briefing," he checked his watch. "In just about an hour. Take some time. Get settled in. The conference room is on this floor. CS-1001. Down the hallway we came through. Make a right. You can't miss it."

Tom nodded.

"I'll find it."

"Great." Fontaine stepped toward the door. "Ms. Green will be facilitating. She doesn't like people to be late." He paused for a moment. "You know what? I'll make sure someone is here to guide you to the conference room."

"Kelly Green will be running the briefing?"

Fontaine nodded.

"You know our ops manager?"

It was Tom's turn to nod. "We worked together a number of years ago. I'm starting to wonder if she's the reason I was given this assignment."

David Fontaine just looked at him, still seated on the loveseat. He regarded the man for a minute and then shrugged.

"I don't know what to tell you, Tom." He smiled and pulled open the door. "I've always known her to get what she wants, so if she wanted you on this mission, I'm sure that's why you're here."

He pulled the door fully open and took one step outside. He stopped and looked back into the small passenger cabin.

"You know," he said, grinning – only with his mouth. His eyes remained cold. "If she personally put you on this mission, I'm feeling better about our chances of success than I was before."

He nodded at Tom, stepped all the way into the corridor, and let the door hiss shut behind him.

"Hey," Tom said to the now-closed door. "That's great."

**

Tom had found the map and diagrams buried within his huge stack of mission paperwork after Fontaine left. Epsilon Complex, the main structure, was three floors – including the top deck. Those three floors shared many areas including the helicopter landing spaces, a submersible dive deck, crew quarters, equipment storage, a galley and a hospital. Scattered throughout this were three main divisions of the actual work being performed at the complex.

Section 1: Data analysis and storage.

Section 2: Communications and operations.

Section 3: Research and history.

The second stage of the facility, the piece that was tethered and hanging below the big structure, was largely Section 4: Observation and experimentation. All told, there were about 100 people scuttling to and fro completing any number of tasks for the tech conglomerate that paid their salaries.

**

The briefing was held in a large meeting room situated in a corner of the lower level of the facility. One wall was the door and numerous whiteboards. The other wall was a huge video screen and two more smaller whiteboards flanking it. The other two walls were windows looking out at the ocean horizon. With the sun setting, the vista was quite beautiful. They were too far away from Ross Island to see it without equipment, but the waves and clouds more than made up for it. Fontaine ushered Tom into the room. There were already three people in there.

"Tom," Fontaine said, pointing to person after person. "This is Archer, head of Section 2. This is Cami, head of Section 1." He pointed to the final person in the room who had moved to stand in front of the big monitor. "And you know Kelly Green, our operations manager." He grinned and nodded at the middle-aged blonde. "Don't worry. She's heard all the jokes already."

"It's good to see you again, Tom," Kelly said, smiling.

Tom nodded and smiled as well.

"Same. I didn't realize you were at this facility when I accepted the gig."

"Oh," she said, furrowing her brow. "It wasn't meant to be a surprise. I was clear with them. I'm sorry. You must feel like you were ambushed."

Tom shook his head.

"Not at all," he said. "Not ambushed. Shocked a little. But it's all good. I'm here to help."

Kelly nodded. "Great. That's great to hear. Everyone, please." She gestured at the room that she was ready to get started.

Facing the monitor were three large rectangular tables each situated with four chairs. The members of the group found their way to an open seat. As per his custom, Tom chose a seat that was front-and-center to the action. His goal was to learn as much as possible in the shortest time possible. He unloaded the messenger bag and grabbed his clipboard – the one he had been making notes on during the discussion with Fontaine in his quarters.

"There'll be time to do a proper meet-and-greet in a few minutes," Kelly said. "So you can all get to know our high-priced consultant. Over dinner. I'm sure you haven't eaten anything, Tom, since McMurdo. For right now, we're going to supplement your files with the video record and whatever background you might need. There will be a planning session bright and early tomorrow morning. We'll present the plans we've come up with and seek any input you might have from your objective first impressions. Fair enough?"

"Fire away," Tom said.

**

Kelly Green picked up a small computer tablet from the front table. It was something of a remote control for the large monitor as the big screen came to life immediately.

A menu screen came up with eleven boxes lined up in it.

"These represent the eleven drone missions that have so far been run," she said, sliding a cursor in the shape of an open hand around the screen. "Ten successful missions and one failure. You can watch all these at your leisure, but here's the final mission of this particular drone." She clicked the icon for Mission 11 and stepped away from the monitor to give Tom a clear view.

Tom could see that the full video was close to an hour long, but Kelly had cued up the final three minutes. The screen was showing the audience what the drone had *seen* through the main camera in the front of the unit. There were various icons and readouts along the margins of the screen listing out numerous factors including speed, water pressure, elapsed mission time, depth and the like. One note caught his attention – Remote Access Disabled.

"Could these units be controlled remotely?" he asked Kelly as well as the room. "I understood them to be self-driven. AI-piloted, right?"

Kelly shook her head. "That feature has not yet been enabled. There were glitches. The developers at DARPA as well as a team at Allied Genetics are working on it."

Tom made a note on his pad of paper.

The video continued and the audience could see that the drone was taking measurements just passing the 9,000-foot mark. The screen had almost no natural light and was only illuminated by the powerful ring light that wrapped around the drone as well as the six strong headlamps arranged around the body. Kelly paused the video and highlighted a section like a professional sports announcer might do on a television broadcast.

"This shadow **here** caught our attention," she said, pointing to the monitor where she had circled a section in yellow. "At first it looked like just that … a shadow. A shimmer. The undulation of the water. But I'll rock twenty frames back and forth and you can see that it's deliberate movement."

It was only a second or two forward and then backward over and over again, but Tom was watching intently. He could certainly see what looked like a large object on an intercept trajectory with the drone.

"Is this a trick of the mind?" he again asked the room. "We know something happened, so we're, like, seeing something that might not necessarily be there. Pareidolia?"

"You're referring to the concept of seeing faces in random objects? Like matrixing?" Cami responded. She was sitting in the chair behind and to the right of Tom. "I thought about that, too. I don't think so, mostly because of what happens next."

Kelly nodded and pressed play again on the video. It was only another forty-five seconds until the attack came.

"Whoa," Tom said. "Rewind that. Slow it down."

She was ready and likely had gone through this same process a dozen or so times. Kelly backed the footage up and hit an icon to drop the playback to .25x. A quarter of the normal video speed. Tom stood up and walked to the front of the table, leaned his butt against the edge and crossed his arms in front of the big monitor.

Frame by frame a huge black shape came into view, swooped around and bit down on the tail section of the drone. There was no sound, but the visuals coming from the drone's forward camera shook violently. Kelly paused the playback and moved it backward frame by frame. She stopped at the best image they had captured from the sea creature that had attacked the small submersible.

Tom leaned in.

The mouth was enormous and was the first noticeable feature of the image. It was easily large enough to completely swallow the drone. Clearly, the decision to bite the AI machine was a conscious one. The next thing he saw was the teeth. If the mouth was a sideways oval, the teeth ringed the extreme top and bottom of the void. With no comparison, it was impossible to tell the exact size, but based on the size of the drone, the teeth could have been two feet long from gums to tip.

Tom shuddered.

The next thing he noticed about the image was the eyes. If the skin of the beast was a deep purple, the eyes were black and glassy. And there were four of them – two on either side of the head.

"Predator eyes," Tom said to himself.

"Excuse me?" Kelly asked, the closest to him.

Tom uncrossed his arms and pointed to the section of the monitor.

"The shape and spacing of the eyes," he said. "The fact that they are deeper set behind a protective ridge. These are evolutionary cues that this is the face of a predator. This beast is not protecting its territory, but hunting."

"Interesting."

"They look slightly human," Fontaine said as if noticing the eyes for the first time.

"That's because human eyes are considered predator eyes," Tom said, leaning back to the table and crossing his arms anew. "The almond shape, spaced closer to the edges of the face, deeper set within the orbital bone. We evolved to hunt and kill. Office jobs are a relatively new addition to our evolutionary cycle."

Everyone was quiet, looking at him.

"Okay," Kelly said, turning back to the big monitor and making some adjustments on her computer tablet. "We know from later footage, the creature clamped down on the rear half of the drone – smashing it nearly flat as if it was an empty soda can." She pressed the icon for "play" on her control pad and the image lurched forward again.

Tom first noticed the warbling lights as the outer shell of the drone was compromised and malfunctioning. The screen readout confirmed this as there were error warnings and blinking red text covering numerous spots where there were relaxed, professional readouts only moments earlier. The entire image shivered yet again, and the drone began a journey of lateral movement. It was as if something had grabbed it and was now pushing the object sideways toward the wall of the ice chimney.

"Based on later evidence," Kelly said again, slowing down the footage slightly, "we believe that the anomaly clamped down on the drone and pushed it downward and outward until it reached the horizontal cave about a quarter of a mile below them at the point of initial impact."

"That's where the Galbreath found it? In the cave?"

Kelly nodded.

"Correct. Eventually, the damage reached the calamitous stage and the drone shut down," she continued, turning to look at the screen. They had a brief glimpse of the mouth of the tunnel from above as the monster powered down toward it with the drone in its mouth. It had a small battery reserve for a distress signal. That's eventually how we found it in the cave."

**

The image on the screen froze, as Kelly looked down at the control pad. She began manipulating commands and the video melted into the selection screen which melted into the master database. She had backed away from the drone footage and selected a file called N802 Galbreath Final. She hovered over and then double-clicked it through the touchpad. Another video opened. There were no images, yet, but Tom could see that it was presented differently than the drone footage. The screen was broken up into quadrants.

On her control pad, Kelly selected from a menu system and status timeline at the bottom of the four videos each advanced about forty-five minutes. There was a rush of super-speed images on all four screens while the cursor fast-forwarded to the selected timestamp. The top left image was labeled as the FWD CAM and showed a view of the water illuminated by three high-powered beams of light. The top right image was REAR CAM and showed essentially the same image as the first cam … however, it was clear that this was looking from the aft of the vessel. The bottom left image was the interior of the craft. It was labeled CRW CBN and showed the three men sitting at their assigned stations. The bottom right image was the BEL CAM and looked to be pointing straight down from the belly of the Galbreath.

Each of the four cameras were ringed with data, stats and measurements. When Tom looked closer, he could see that they were all identical. The four cameras were looking at different things but were recording the same metric data.

"So this is a failure of the team," Tom said, still standing, leaning forward. He reached around behind him and grabbed his pad of paper to make some notes. "The crew. They ignored the proximity alarms."

On the four screens, the Galbreath was zeroing in on the downed drone and winching it up to the belly of the vessel. It was the first time Tom could see the damage that the big drone sustained. The rear half was smashed, and the rest of the body was covered in holes from where the monster – "anomaly" as Kelly called it – had bitten into the hull and dragged it into the tunnel.

"We believe they had silenced the alarms thinking it was the tracking system alerting them to the drone's presence," Kelly said, her tone perhaps tinged with a little defensiveness. "Unfortunately, the proximity alarms took over the same channel as the drone's distress call."

She paused for a moment.

"It's a programming glitch."

The Galbreath crew had secured the drone and reversed out of the tunnel. After a few quiet moments there was sudden chaos. The only warning onscreen was one crewman grabbing the armrests of his seat in terror and then everything went to hell. Since the cabin camera was stabilized, there was no sense of exactly what happened. To the viewers of the footage, however, it looked as if the world was suddenly thrown sideways and then began to roll. They could tell this mainly because the man, Johnson, rolled around the walls and ceiling of the cabin, striking his head quite violently against the bulkhead right above his seat – where he was ejected.

There was nothing on any of the monitors that showed what struck them.

"Seriously?" Tom asked the room. "All those cameras and we don't see the actual attack?"

Kelly Green simply shook her head.

"We catch a glimpse a little later," she said. "It's clearly the same anomaly from the drone attack."

Tom turned back to the screen. His eyes looked at the two external cameras first and then looked in on the chaos in the cabin. There looked to be leaks of various liquids from numerous pipes running along the perimeter of the room. He could see the hull integrity warnings as the ship attempted to ascend back to Epsilon Complex. Progress, unfortunately, was halted. The Galbreath, much like the drone, was seized and pushed violently to the side wall of the chimney. There was a horrible impact as any loose debris in the cabin was thrown around the room. The Galbreath smashed against the ice wall and was scraped along the rigid surface. Eventually, the warnings around the screen screamed out that now both propulsion systems were offline. Slowly, the submersible started to sink. Tom could see the depth meter increasing quickly.

A hull breach and implosion were imminent. Kelly slowed down the playback again. The forward camera was clearly damaged, but it was still recording along the zig-zag lighting that had been thrown out of alignment.

Johnson was slumped in his chair clearly unconscious from the massive head trauma. Samir and Rodgers, though, were active. Samir was punching instruments all across his control panel trying to get any sort of maneuverability back online. Rodgers was typing feverishly, attempting to collect and transmit all their data back to the command center. Kelly manipulated her controller and the forward camera enlarged to fill the entire screen. It was clearly damaged and was slightly glitchy. Often, static rushed across the screen from top to bottom. Kelly slowed down the playback just as the shadowy figure emerged again out of the depths. It seemed to brush past the Galbreath and glide out into the distance. There, it did a lazy loop and immediately rushed at the vessel. Even with the slower playback, the speed of the beast was incredible. There was another blast of static and Kelly paused the playback as soon as it cleared.

"Jesus Christ," Tom said.

It looked like some sort of eel-shark hybrid. The monster was unexpectedly long with dorsal and ventral fins. The four eyes were closed, essentially, rolled back in a move of self-preservation. The huge oval mouth was just starting to open and Tom could already see the enormous teeth – more like fangs in this image.

Kelly unpaused the image and let the playback run in slow motion. At one-quarter the normal speed, the beast's mouth continued to open to a shocking degree as it kept moving forward toward the sub. Eventually, the screen darkened so much to be useless. It was clear that the anomaly was biting down hard on the vessel. Almost immediately, the screen showed the ERROR red text and then went black. Kelly put the view back to quadrants … and they were all black as well.

The Galbreath had imploded.

"So, what submersibles do you have with offensive capabilities?" Tom asked as he stacked his folders and notepads and butted them against the table.

**

It was the same group of people, but they had moved from the sterile conference room to Kelly's office. She had a corner office with beautiful views, a huge desk and two vinyl club chairs facing the desk. They brought two folding chairs in from storage. Kelly sat behind her desk with Tom and Cami in the club chairs. Fontaine and Archer flanked them in folding chairs.

"I guess I'm curious what your role is here, Mr. Granville," Cami said, folding her hands across her lap, resting atop the tablet computer she had taken notes on during the briefing. "Ms. Green's seal of approval means a lot, but as my team will be providing support, I'd like to know how you fit into all that."

Tom nodded. He had been warned that there might be some resistance. Not a lot. Some.

"I can't get into the details," he said, a diplomatic smile oozing across his face. "I've done work for the two concerned organizations in the past. Allied Genetics. DARPA. Since both are ass-deep in Epsilon Complex, I was sent as an advance scout-slash-problem solver on their behalf. Figure out what's going on down below us. Kill it. Capture it. Whatever. Make sure you don't lose any more equipment worth tens of millions of dollars. If you want to kill a monster, you need to send a bigger monster." He paused for a moment, the smile never leaving his face. "So, I'm here. Clear enough?"

"I was told to give you whatever help I could, so," Cami said, trailing off and leaving the intended question hang in the air.

"I'm still collecting data," Tom said, leaning back in his chair. "But it seems pretty obvious that we're eventually going to have to go on a hunt. You've already lost two crafts – the manned submersible Galbreath and the remote-AI research drone vessel. I'd prefer our losses to end there."

"As would we all," Kelly said, clearing her throat. "You asked about offensive weapons. Two of our manned subs are equipped offensively. Torpedoes – both lightweight and heavyweight – as well as depth charges. They are also equipped with radio-controlled cannons that fire supercavitating ammunition."

"Really? A DARPA design?"

"Based on a DSG concept paired with a magnetic rail-gun-firing mechanism," Kelly nodded. "The cannons aren't all that accurate underwater, but they pack a wallop."

There was a bit of a pause. Tom got the sense that the three section heads were not fully aware of these measures.

"The *August* and the *Hariwulf*?" Fontaine said, leaning forward. "Is that why they've been off-limits? Samir wanted to take the Hariwulf but you fought him. Did he know it had offensive capabilities?"

Kelly thought for a moment.

"Yes, he knew. They are still being tested, though," Kelly said. "Not approved for mission-use."

"That's going to change right now," Tom said. "Put a team on them. Get them depth-ready. Fins-up first thing in the morning," he said, grinning, standing and looping the canvas messenger bag across his chest in one practiced move.

"Okay, I approve," Kelly said. "Team, you'll get a logistics report in an hour. You're dismissed. Tom, hang back a sec."

**

Tom assumed he was going to get reprimanded for overstepping a boundary, so he remained standing, leaning back against a large bookcase filled with reference manuals. He crossed his arms and hefted an eyebrow.

For her part, Kelly walked around the side of her desk and leaned her rear against the leading edge. In fact, she lifted herself up and fully sat on the desktop, gently swinging her feet beneath her. She looked at Tom and smiled.

"Oh, relax," she laughed. "It's good to see you, Tom. I just wanted to chat for a minute. How've you been?"

Tom slumped his shoulders and gave a bit of a relaxed sigh.

"Whew," he said, grinning back at her and pulling a chair over to sit in. "Earlier, I spoke without thinking. The situation was not mine to take control of."

Kelly nodded.

"Yeah," she said. "You're probably right. But you weren't wrong. I was getting to the same conclusion as you. We're going to have to go back down … and this time take a bigger gun."

Tom nodded.

"Yep."

"So, what's been going on? I haven't seen you since the Anselmo consultancy."

Tom nodded.

"Yeah," he said. "It's been a while." He leaned back in the chair and rubbed his hands over his face, taking care to squeeze his palms into his eye sockets. It was something of a nervous tic, but also a clue that he was starting to grow a headache. "That was a good gig. Anselmo."

"Only because you saved my ass," Kelly said, losing her grin for the first time. She pursed her eyebrows together. "You found that system glitch well before I did … and just in the nick of time, if I recall correctly. Saved the company something like four billion dollars according to the last estimate."

"Pish posh," Tom said and laughed. "Right place. Right time."

Kelly, too, laughed.

"Be that as it may," she continued, "I owe you one."

The silence in the room became stifling. Tom leaned forward in his chair and rubbed the stubble on his chin. He cracked his neck from side to side and looked back at Kelly – who hadn't moved since last speaking.

"Heroux," he said, clearing his throat.

"You got there in one," Kelly said. "I knew you were down and thought we could team up again. Solve my sea monster problem and put you back on the plus side of the ledger."

"I'm 18 and 1 by my count, Kelly," Tom said. "But you're right. Heroux was a big failure." He paused for a moment, slouching in his chair. Kelly leaned forward from her perched position. She didn't say anything – just let him stew for a bit. "Heroux Logistics was working on a big government contract. Defense budget. They were working on some sort of," he waved his hand dismissively, as if to indicate that he was going to skip over the greater details of the business. "Some sort of biomechanical weapon. Things began to go a little weird and I was brought on to clean it up. Acting as a project manager-slash-efficiency expert. Long story short, we couldn't eliminate the problem in time. Some people died. And, yet, I still got paid."

He fell silent for a moment.

"I've been trying to make up for it ever since."

Kelly thought for a moment, reading into what was just said.

"You weren't blacklisted," she said. Tom shook his head.

"No, not really. Officially, the gig was a success. We found the problem and fixed it. It was just a little too late. I was still getting work. Just nothing big. I've been atoning. Dead bodies have a way of following you in reports. Paperwork. Hidden between the lines. What's **not** said." He fell silent yet again. "I keep looking for that job where I can solve something and prevent the catastrophic failure. Like in the old days."

She smiled at that.

"Like in the old days," she said. "Well, I'm already down a drone, a sub, and three team members. You'd be doing me a huge favor if we can stop the bleeding right now."

Tom nodded and stood up from his chair.

"You got it, Kelly." He turned to leave the office and she called him back when his hand hit the door handle.

"You're planning on diving tomorrow."

"Damn straight," he said and left.

CHAPTER TWO
AS ABOVE, SO BELOW

CAMI CAUGHT UP WITH TOM after he had left Kelly's office. She had waited in the corridor, a few paces away from the door. Had Tom turned left out of the office, he would have walked right past her. Instead, though, he turned right and Cami had to chase him down just a bit.

"I'm not naïve," she said to his back in an effort to get him to stop, which he did. "I was brought on as a data tech section head, but I knew there was heavy military involvement. They didn't just *donate* the drones to us; they were *looking* for something."

Tom slid his hands into the pockets of his slacks and leaned against an interior wall of the hallway. "Looking for what, exactly?"

Cami stood about five feet in front of him, not leaning on the wall. She was standing flat-footed in the hallway with her arms crossed. She thought for a moment and then shrugged.

"I'm not sure," she said. "We know the Ice Chimney is a natural phenomenon but ... I don't know. I suppose government agencies are always curious, I guess."

"Have they been directing their own experiments? Are there any reps from DARPA onboard?"

Cami shook her head.

"I'm not exactly on *those* email distribution lists," she said. "There's always strange stuff going on. Though that's not unusual. Given our location at the bottom of the Earth – and our situation, exploring a never-before-seen natural phenomenon … you can imagine there're a lot of divergent personalities on Epsilon. Both of them."

She got silent for a moment, pensive. Tom could see the crinkle across her brow intensify.

"I did catch wind of something called **Operation Deep Zone**, or something like that. Not on our official manifests."

"Interesting," Tom said and paused. "How many probe missions have been run?"

"That's more of a Section 2 thing," she said. "But there could have been twenty or twenty-five missions before everything was shut down a couple days ago."

Interesting, Tom thought. *That's not what Fontaine said. Why would he lie?*

To Cami he said: "Have they been bringing back samples?"

"Sure," she said. "Sea life. Wall scrapings. That sort of thing."

"Have they been able to reach the bottom yet?"

"We don't think we're even close," Cami said. "But it's just a guess."

"I see," he said, shoving off from the wall and continuing on his original path. Cami walked beside him. "You mentioned **both** Epsilons."

"Sure," she said. "You've been briefed, right? Above us might look like an oil derrick but it's really more like a giant, square barge, held in place by continuous monitoring and propulsion. Epsilon

Complex. Think of it like a three-story corporate office. Tethered beneath is the true observation deck. Epsilon Prime. Think of it like the deep science laboratory. All the main launches come from up here. Prime is about a third the size and is a series of labs. That's where all the samples are."

"Huh," Tom said. "I guess I'll have to take a look."

**

"You're doing that just to piss me off, right?" Jonah Marek casually brushed a small pile of paperwork off the corner of his desk and let the folders and clipboards clatter to the floor. "I mean, you can't be this intentionally stupid."

The young researcher, Tina, bent to pile up the scattered papers and pick them back up. Marek waited for her to finish and stand before he also dropped the file he was holding in his hand – making her bend again to clean it up.

"You need to run those numbers again, fix every graph and correct the typo on page seventeen."

Marek sighed and turned back to look at his desk. He heard the quiet in the lab surrounding him.

"Back to work," he said quietly, without turning his head.

**

While the lab was officially called Epsilon Prime on the corporate documentation, most of those familiar with the complex simply called it the "Puck." It wasn't a particularly creative nickname because that's what the structure looked like – a giant hockey puck. Big, black, perfectly circular. The only difference was that the Puck was ringed with huge windows so the lab could carry out its primary function as a deep-sea observation facility.

In the current configuration, the Puck was actually "Section 4," and Jonah Marek was the chief.

Even though Marek believed himself to be a brilliant researcher and a damn-good manager, the truth is that he was lucky. He seemed to have an innate, unexpressed ability to surround himself with driven geniuses who somehow thrived under his substandard management. It was a paradox that Allied Genetics couldn't explain or replicate. With his poor attitude and natural ability to demean his team, Marek was on a short list of department heads that could be replaced at a moment's notice – if only it was that easy. His department continued to excel and deliver outstanding results.

Jonah stood from the small workstation and walked across the floor to the closest lab. No one involved in their own work paid him any attention.

"What are you working on, rookie?" Marek entered the lab to see three people working at well-lit stations. He had focused his ire on one young man.

"Good afternoon, sir," the rookie – Jason – said, turning from the table and looking over his right shoulder. "Geology, sir. We're examining rock samples from mission eight."

All three researchers were dressed similar to surgeons or, more precisely, pathologists. Heavy white scrubs, a thick apron, latex gloves, goggles and N95 ventilated masks. Marek wore none of this gear save for a pair of goggles he had strapped on his face before coming in the room. As he looked around, he noticed the other two researchers were working with rocks of various sizes. Some were being cleaned, some were being measured and photographed, some were being probed. This is what Jason was doing. In fact, he looked to be examining a tiny crevasse with what looked like dental tools.

"Exciting," Marek said. He looked away from Jason and wandered around the room. The rookie went back to work, his hands shaking just a bit due to the stress of having the boss *right there*.

Crack.

Marek turned on his heel and looked at the rookie.

"What the hell was that?"

The boss stomped back over to the workstation to see what had happened. He was at first worried that the idiot researcher had broken a delicate piece of equipment, but quickly saw that was not the case. The large stone now sat in two halves on the table.

"I, uh, I don't know what happened," the rookie held his hands palms up, fingers splayed on either side of the broken stone. He held two of the small dental instruments – one in each hand. "I was cleaning what looked like a small crack in the surface and the stone split apart. It's hollow inside. Like two cereal bowls glued together."

The half of the stone on the right was still wobbling a bit as it was finding its balance on the smooth, lighted surface.

"Hollow," Marek repeated.

He leaned in closer to the table. The other two researchers had joined him standing behind the rookie.

"There looks to be a pooled liquid in this half," a lady researcher said over the rookie's left shoulder. "Almost like mercury."

"There sure is," Marek said. "Get a syringe, scoop it out, find out what it is."

**

After the briefing, Tom had eaten dinner with the section heads who were in attendance. He was putting together some background information on each of them. Personality stuff. They all seemed pleasant enough in their own ways. He had then retired, alone, to his quarters. He planned to read through the pertinent information again – as well as his notes so far from the adventure – and then try to get some sleep. He could never sleep sitting up – so the forty hours or so since he left the mainland on an airplane had been forty wakeful hours. He was exhausted.

**

In the morning, the mission was going to leave in an hour. Tom would go as an observer. He had to argue that one and pull rank on Green to make it happen – especially after the recent disaster. In fact, he was unsure why it was so important that he went along. A tingle at the base of his brain was telling him that he should go and he had learned years ago to listen to that small voice. Plus, he was set on taking any opportunity … any chance … at redemption. He had planned since he got the phone call that this would be the mission that redeemed him.

The dive would comprise three vehicles – the offensive-weaponed Hariwulf would be flanked by two drones. The drones would act as high-speed sentries – both for advance warning and possible decoys. The Hariwulf would have a crew of five plus the onlooker Tom Granville. Right now, Tom was being led around the sub by the pilot, Jones, as he pointed out the various features. Engines, backup engines, depth charge chutes, cannons, torpedoes.

"Huh," Tom said in surprise.

They rounded the corner around the stubby starboard wing of the sub.

"What is it?" Jones asked. The man had originally shook Tom's hand and introduced himself as Calamari Jones, but the consultant had silently vowed that he would never call him that.

"I guess I didn't see that paintjob before," Tom said.

"Oh yeah," Jones said, smiling. "I had that added when we started outfitting her with all the guns. Seemed appropriate."

Around the nose of the sub, they had painted a shark's mouth – open, full of dangerously sharp teeth. It reminded Tom of the aggressive paintjob of many military aircraft – fighters from as early as WWI. Not that the fake mouths ever instilled fear in the enemy, it was more a psychological edge for the airmen – the fighting spirit. Like someone might feel more confident when they were wearing an expensive jacket. The custom paint job is really only there for morale.

"I get that," Tom said, smiling back. "I suppose the shark teeth are more appropriate on a submersible than a fighter plane, too." Tom thought for a moment. "Do they usually do that on military subs, too? Or just planes?"

Jones shook his head.

"Nah. It would actually work against a sub for a few reasons." They had stopped walking and Jones leaned against the nose of the vessel while he ticked off the three points on the fingers of his right hand. "First, subs are generally coated in radar/sound-absorbing paint so a giant painted face on the nose of the craft would add vulnerability. It would also make the sub immediately identifiable. And third, I suppose, is just the waste of resources. You gotta spend time while the craft is in dry dock giving it a custom paint job … and then touch it up every time because seawater is quite corrosive. Waste of time and money."

"Sure. That all makes sense."

"I thought so," Jones said. "Let's get you over to gear and get you fitted for your suit."

Jones clapped Tom on the shoulder and turned him to a far corner of the dive deck.

"You know what I just found out," Jones said as they had walked away.

"Couldn't begin to guess," Tom said.

"They call it a pound cake because of the ingredients, not the weight of the finished product. You see, the recipe is easy. Four ingredients. A pound of flour. A pound of sugar. A pound of butter. A pound of eggs."

"Really?"

"Sure thing. Yeah. I think a pound of eggs is generally ten eggs. And you can juice a couple oranges or lemons for flavor, but the logic is the same."

"That's … interesting, Jones. Thanks for that."

"Yep," he said and steered Tom toward a door in the corner of the big room. "We're over here."

**

It was essentially a huge locker room. There was a smaller gear office in the corner that stored spare equipment and that's where Tom went to get his wetsuit. They wouldn't be leaving the Hariwulf, but it was standard operating procedure as the Epsilon wetsuits contained biometric sensors as well as a few other tricks. The other four members of the crew were already getting dressed and Jones joined them. When Tom had collected his gear, he walked over and inserted himself into the larger group.

Calamari Jones smiled and started introducing the other members of the crew.

"Manning the 68G1 Hariwulf will be yours truly at the helm," he said, then pointing at each person in turn, "Marya will be my second in command coordinating comms and tech reach. Ellis and Goldberg will both be watching over sonar contact and weapons. Cashlin will maintain sub systems, data and sonar monitoring."

They had all made their version of acknowledgement which was either a head nod, a crooked smile or finger guns.

"This is Tom Granville," Jones continued. "He's a consultant on loan to us from our betters. He has plenty of experience ... but nothing that'll necessarily help him in the Big Icy." Jones clapped Tom on the back in an older-brotherly-way, smiling the entire time.

"It's a pleasure to meet you all," Tom said. "I'm strictly here as an observer. Let me know if I get in your way. No need to walk on eggshells, here."

"Oh," Goldberg said with a grin. "We weren't planning to."

CHAPTER THREE
BETWEEN THE DEVIL AND THE
DEEP BLUE SEA

THE HARIWULF WAS LARGER THAN THE GALBREATH, but it was a cramped interior with a full crew plus one. Jones and his team were going through their various pre-dive checklists onboard the sub. The comms team – with both the department head Archer and the operations manager Kelly Green in attendance – were likewise going through a detailed check. There was a steady stream of chatter going back and forth from the sub, Section 2 and the Puck. Everyone was nervous and trying to be hyper-professional in light of the recent disaster. The Galbreath crew was well-known and beloved among the team … their tragic and mysterious passing had not yet been absorbed at Epsilon on an emotional level.

"Pre-check complete, Hariwulf," came the voice from the control room. "You are cleared for dive."

"Copy," Jones said.

There was a green blinking light on the control surface at the front of the sub – a visual indicator of their *clear ready* status. Marya reached over from her command chair next to Jones's and clicked it shut.

"Acknowledged," she said to both the control room and the sub crew at the same time. She looked at Jones and nodded.

They strapped in as did the rest of the crew-plus-Tom. When everyone was secure, Jones turned back to look at the main instrument panel.

"Engaging dive, base. Hariwulf is go."

Tom's stomach turned as the sub tilted forward and nosed down at a 45-degree angle. They had, seconds before, been looking at the horizon just above the choppy Antarctic Ocean morning waves. Now, the front third of the sub was dunked under the water's surface. It was disorienting for the observer, but he smiled at the new experience. With a shocking suddenness, the clamps holding the Hariwulf in place released and the engines turned on two seconds later. The vessel shot into the frigid water like a bullet.

The internal lights dimmed, and the external floodlights came on at the same time. Tom was straining forward to look out the massive windows covering the front of the sub. He could see the darkness of the water below them, the gentle glow of the lights from the visible portion of Epsilon Complex and the grim shadow of the Puck 200 feet below them. Thirty seconds into their dive, they saw the two drones that were set to join them on the adventure. They were on a matching downward course, slightly ahead and flanking the big sub.

"Ah, our friends have arrived," Jones said and smiled.

"Visual confirmation of drones A and B," Marya said over comms. "Tracking algorithm loaded."

"Copy that, Hariwulf," came the response from the control room.

"Passing 2,500 feet," Cashlin said from the rear of the sub. She sat across from Tom and looked over at him to smile. Tom returned the smile. "Mr. Granville," she said after a moment. "Did they tell you just how big the Ice Chimney is?"

Tom simply shook his head in response.

"It's nearly a perfect circle," she continued. "The diameter of which is just over 400 feet. About 125 percent the length of a football field. We estimate that it could be around 30,000 feet deep, but we've not been down that far. That it's called the Ice Chimney is a bit of a misnomer. As you can see, the walls are rock. I think the nickname comes from the Ross Ice Shelf and the freezing waters of the South Ocean."

"Interesting," Tom said.

"Many species live in the area," Goldberg started. "We've witnessed octopi, spider crabs and a few different kinds of mackerel sharks … namely the mako. Oh, and orcas. Killer whales. Although in these waters their black and white skin is generally covered with a thin film of plankton, so they look more brownish and yellowish. It was strange the first time I saw them."

"Again, interesting," Tom said, trying to soak all the information in at once. He turned from first looking at Cashlin over to Goldberg and then back out the front windows of the Hariwulf. Any vestige of light from the surface had long disappeared. He could only see by virtue of the sub's spotlights and the lights of the two drones. It was surreal. The water was mostly clear, but the chunks of debris and small organisms rushing past the cockpit window was disorienting. It wasn't too dissimilar from driving in a snowstorm. At night.

"Passing 7,500 feet," Cashlin called out.

"Slow descent by twenty percent," Jones said.

"Copy that," Marya said. "Slowing descent by twenty percent."

Jones turned his chair to look at Tom.

"Did you realize that in certain conditions a human's sense of smell is actually stronger than a shark's?" He paused for effect. "You've heard the term *petrichor*?"

Tom shook his head.

"It refers to the smell of dirt, grass, trees ... the Earth ... after the rain. It's a heavy, meaty smell. We are tied to the Earth, you see. The human ability to recognize this smell is actually greater than a shark's ability to smell blood in the water. Humans can sense petrichor at five parts per trillion. That's somewhere around 200,000 times more sensitive than the shark and blood. Cool, right?"

"I had no idea we were so amazing," Tom said, grinning.

"Petrichor's not going to save us down here," Marya added. "Sir."

**

"Passing 10-k, sir," Cashlin said.

"Back 'er down just a bit more," Jones said. "We're coming up on the horizontal shaft," the captain said seemingly for Tom's benefit. Tom's only response was a slight nod.

"Nothing on our sensors," Ellis said, peering only at his bank of monitors. "Nothing on the extended range of the drones."

"Copy that," Marya said. "Control, any weirdness up there?"

"Negative, Hariwulf. We're not picking anything up."

"Roger," Jones said. "Let's check out this tunnel."

He pulled the sub to a hover about ninety feet from the mouth of the cave, still flanked by the two drones.

"High-def scans, impact lights, full-spectrum analysis," he called to the crew. "Let's hit it with everything we can. Marya, simultaneous feed to control."

"Simultaneous feed, sir. Copy that."

While everyone else was hammering away at their keyboards and sensor equipment, Tom stood up and walked to the front of the vessel, his eyes never leaving the big windows and the enormous tunnel entrance. The edges were barely lit by the high-powered floodlights of the Hariwulf, Drone A and Drone B.

"Rough circle," Ellis said. "Just about a width of … um … looks like sixty-three feet at its widest. Maybe fifty feet tall."

"Copy that," Jones said. "Keep scanning. Three minutes and we power in."

"Aye, sir," Marya said.

"Damn," Tom said, standing right behind Captain "Calamari" Jones.

"Yep," Jones said. "That's something you don't see every day."

**

They proceeded slowly, but still made it to the original drone's crash site in just a few minutes. They were 200 feet from the mouth of the tunnel and could see the deep grooves on the floor of the cave where the punctured drone crashed and slid to a halt. Of course, there was nothing there because the Galbreath had carried it back into the Ice Chimney … but the evidence remained.

"Nothing on external," Ellis called. He was looking at a smaller monitor in his bay. They had left Drone A at the mouth of the cave scanning the sinkhole, guarding their rear flank.

Ping.

All eyes went to Ellis.

"I'm getting some faint movement," he said, bending forward at the waist looking at his screen and the text readout along the right side of the sonar image. "Ahead and to the right. Five hundred feet. It stopped."

"Stopped?" Tom asked.

"Aye. One faint ping and then nothing. I have its position marked, but the signal is gone."

The captain nodded and turned back to the front widows of the submersible.

"All ahead half, Marya."

"Aye aye," she said. "High alert."

The Hariwulf, escorted by one of the big drones, powered away from giant claw marks that the half-crushed drone made into the dirt floor of the cavern as it slid to a destroyed stop. Marya pressed some keys on her control console and the drone moved ahead until it was about ninety feet in front of them.

"Cashlin," she said. "Keep an eye on Drone A. Let me know if anything comes into the mouth of the cave."

"Roger that."

Jones and Marya leaned forward, even if subconsciously, and peered out the large center window in the middle of the bow of the sub. The rest of the team clicked and tightened their seatbelt harnesses. Tom, seeing this, did the same in his passenger chair. He noticed that Jones had a nervous tic of clearing his throat every couple minutes. It was a small, subtle thing, but it was a monster tell – something that Tom would have picked up in a half dozen hands of Texas Hold'em. Clearly, the man was nervous.

The Hariwulf had nearly a dozen powerful LED spotlights illuminating the area around them. They could see the drone leading the way, but it was on the edge of their visibility. This far beneath the surface and this far into a lightless cave … it was like trying to look through a field of ink.

Jones cleared his throat.

"Control, do you read us?"

There was a brief burst of static that seemed to swallow the few words of a response. Either Epsilon Complex could read them but could not transmit with all the interference or they couldn't hear the message and were asking for clarification. Either way, they were on their own. Jones looked at Marya.

"Make sure we're forcing a continuous data transfer," he said.

She nodded and looked over her shoulder. "Cashlin?"

"On it," she said. "Sir."

The drone maintained the same distance and speed in front of the big sub. Jones cleared his throat after three more minutes.

"Hang on," Ellis said. "Contact. Dead ahead right. About fifty feet in front of the drone."

"Copy that," Jones said, leaning forward even further in his chair. They would have visual confirmation of the SONAR signal in mere minutes.

"Uh oh," Ellis said, and Marya spun in her chair. "The contact has split."

"Split?" she said.

"It was one contact and then it suddenly became … more. I can't get an accurate read. Somewhere between ten and twenty."

"They were clustered in a pod," Cashlin offered, looking at her own screen … a playback of what Ellis had seen on scope. "And then split up."

"Weapons ready," Jones said. "High alert. Lock your aim, but don't fire unless there is a clear danger."

"Copy," replied Ellis and Goldberg. The two men recalibrated their viewscreens and pulled what looked like a video game joystick from the side of the panel. "Cannons loose."

The suddenness of the attack was staggering.

**

The majority of the employees on Epsilon Complex were distracted by the mission. Some were curious about what the exploratory mission might find. Most were curious simply because of how the previous mission ended – in the worst kind of failure. Researchers who were on shift found their way to monitor the progress either through a pop-up window on their computer screens or listening to mission reports on carefully concealed earbuds. Not that the leadership as a whole would have dissuaded them from following along. Project loyalty was important.

Researchers off-shift, however, made sure to find their way to mission control, monitoring consoles or the huge window observatories on the Puck – just for a glimpse of the Hariwulf coming back to base.

Jonah Marek stalked around the Puck, however, on his own mission. He couldn't be bothered with the in-progress mission. It was after the mission where his team would be asked to shine. They weren't mission critical; they were excavation examination.

And experimentation.

One part of Section 4 was essentially a cubicle farm with a dozen or more researchers glued to high-powered computers poring over data and various mission analytics. As workers saw him coming around, they minimized all non-essential tabs. Even though the company hadn't expressly forbid anyone from following the kill depth mission, the general consensus was that Marek would react poorly to what he considered a distracted workforce.

The boss finally stopped when he reached his destination. A cube like all the others. A minimal amount of personal decorations. Here, a birthday card. There, a slip of printed paper with a stylized font *No Pressure; No Diamonds*. Here, a handwritten page of text. Maybe something personal or inspiring.

"Idiot," Marek hissed.

Marek looked up and around the room, following the path with his eyes that he had just walked. Looking for something he had missed.

"Where's the rookie?" he asked the room in general, not louder than a conversational question.

There was a moment of silence as the researchers were trying to figure out how best to answer and avoid the ire of their supervisor. Finally, the young lady sitting in the cube to the right wheeled her chair backward and spun to look at her boss.

"Jason?" she asked.

"How should I know?" Marek responded. "Yeah. Sure. Jason. The Rookie."

The young lady shrugged.

"I haven't seen him all day, Mr. Marek. He might be sick."

"Sick of hard work," the boss muttered. "Sick of getting a paycheck, too. I should load him into a cannon and fire him back to Russia."

"I don't think Jason is from Russia, Mr. Marek."

"Are you still here?" he asked, walking away from the young researcher. She simply slid her chair back up to her desk and got back to work. These types of outbursts were common in the Puck.

**

There were four "elevators" that propelled workers the 200 feet between the main complex and the research lab. They were arranged at the points of a square overlaid within the observation structure. They ran up and down along thick, tightly-wound cables made of a vinyl-rubber hybrid. It was flexible but retained a high tensile strength. The trip was relatively quick because it was essentially an express elevator with only two stops at the extreme edges.

Marek sat alone in the cart that had six chairs and plenty of standing room.

At his destination, he exited the elevator and walked toward the crew quarters. As a section head, Marek had a keycard that granted him access to every room in the complex. He was only supposed to use it to enter crew quarters when in an extreme emergency.

Someone calling in sick, to him, was an emergency.

The room was nearly completely dark, with nothing but a desk lamp on and various ambient lighting elements – the power indicator of a small television, the ready light on the smoke detector on the ceiling, and so on. Marek heard moaning and hit the switch for the main overhead lights.

"Oh, God."

The room was small. It had space for a twin bed, a desk, small wardrobe and small fridge. Occupants would take advantage of shared restroom facilities – much like the average college dormitory. On the bed, wound up in blankets like a messy burrito, was the sick researcher. The room, though, was ice-cold. The air conditioning unit was running full-blast and there was a small oscillating fan blowing high speed from the desk.

And, then, there was the smell.

"Up and at 'em, doofus," Marek said, stepping into the room. He stopped, however, after a stride and a half. The room reeked of sweat, and he could see the top of Jason's head. His hair was plastered to his scalp – wet – and the pillow was soaked through. What little he could see of the rookie's flesh was red and puffy. Swollen. "Jesus Christ."

Jason's reaction was to pull the blankets even tighter around his face to block out the light. In a rare show of humanity, Marek backed toward the dorm door and flipped the light switch a second time. The room, again, was bathed in darkness. The boss stood there for only another moment.

"Get your shit together, Jason, and get back to work."

Uncharacteristically, he softly closed the door and walked back to the elevator system.

**

They fell from the ceiling of the cavern like a lightning bolt. In the dim edge of the floodlights, it simply looked like 100 long, thin sticks. They fell in a group from the ceiling and surrounded the car-sized drone.

"Weapons free," Ellis said.

"Wait," Marya called. "You'll hit the drone."

"The drone is done-for," Jones said.

They could see the drone sinking to the floor of the cavern. It looked like it was completely covered in a writhing mass of legs that were ripping and tearing at the metal.

"Spider crabs," Jones said.

They looked like giant Japanese spider crabs – but easily twice the size. They had a relatively small body but ten legs, five on each side, that were easily ten feet long. Each tipped with sharp claws. The two front legs, which were another twenty percent longer than the other eight, had massive pinchers.

Both men started firing their weapons and everyone could see the cavitation rounds launching out from beneath both "wings" of the Hariwulf. The rounds weren't accurate at this distance, but they were accurate enough. They punched holes through the bodies of numerous crabs and shredded legs flew away from the downed drone. The floodlights of the drone flickered and failed. There was a moment of quiet.

"Ahem," Jones cleared his throat.

"Do we pursue, sir?" Marya asked.

Jones pursed his brow and thought through his options for just a moment – probably five options in as many seconds.

"Advance on the drone," he said. "Ahead full. Let's see if we can salvage it and take it back to the base for analysis."

"All weapons free," Marya said, pushing the sub forward. "Cashlin, ready the magnetic grapple."

"Copy that."

There was a burst of static over the comms – a destroyed message from Epsilon Complex – but everyone in the vessel jerked in response. An unintentional jump-scare.

"Turn that damn thing down until we get out of this tunnel," the captain said. Marya reached forward and snapped a toggle switch on her control panel. The trailing static of the fractured transmission died away.

The Hariwulf slowly approached the fallen remains of the drone. Unlike the drone almost recovered by the Galbreath, this one left no scorch marks or deep trenches in the packed dirt that acted as the floor of the cavern. It had simply fallen straight down after being disabled. The drone was covered in dents, scratches and broken pieces. There looked to be a dozen deep gouges in numerous parts of the small sub's hull.

There were also a few bullet holes.

"Whoops," Tom said under his breath.

If there was any consolation, it was in the fifteen or so giant crab legs resting around and along the drone on the ground. There were also two dead spider crab bodies.

"They're huge," Marya gasped.

For his part, Jones simply nodded.

The sub continued to slide forward until Cashlin called out from her monitor position. "Hold."

Marya slid the controls from forward, through neutral to reverse and back to neutral to bring the sub to a rest. In position, she hit the control button marked "Hover" and then leaned back to look at Cashlin. She was bent forward in her seat, manning the controls of the magnetic grapple until it had a secure hold of the drone and pulled it up out of the dirt into the underbelly of the big sub.

"Got it."

Marya turned to look at Jones, who sat pensively – staring out the front window. He was pinching his bottom lip from the sides with the thumb and middle finger of his right hand.

"Jones?" Marya asked.

"Backward or forward. Backward or forward." He didn't turn to look at her but was clearly weighing the decision of pursuing the giant spider crabs deeper into the tunnel or calling the mission a waste and returning to base. The decision, though, was made for him in this moment.

"Incoming," Ellis yelled from his mid-ship position.

**

A dozen giant Japanese spider crabs ran into the pooled lights of the Hariwulf with almost no warning. Ellis and Goldberg immediately reached for their weapons controls, but they were too slow. Before the system was activated and they could start firing, six of the ten-foot-tall monsters had launched themselves at the vessel. The sub rocked against its hovering propellers before quickly stabilizing itself.

"Get us out of here," Jones yelled and Marya punched in various commands on her console. The captain reached out and grabbed the steering controls of the submersible. He spun in a quick 180 degree turn and hit full power.

Ellis and Goldberg swiveled the canons to the rear of the sub and began firing at the crabs that were chasing them through the giant tunnel. As soon as they killed one, another took its spot in the formation.

"How many of these damn things are there?" Ellis asked himself.

The sudden motion of the sub had dislodged two of the crabs from the hull, but there were four more out there. Jones could see the arms of one on the starboard side, the two long pinchers visible through the forward window. He could see the arms of another on the port side. He twisted the controls and scraped the port side of the sub against the closest cavern wall. The motion scraped the giant crab from the side of the Hariwulf and Jones pulled the control to the right and headed for the opposite wall to do the same to the other beast.

"Get that drone over here," he said to Marya. "I need a visual out there."

"Copy that."

She punched numerous commands into her console and opened a small picture-in-picture screen across a quadrant of the sub's forward window. It was the forward camera of Drone A coming toward them from the mouth of the cavern.

Cronch.

The Hariwulf scraped against the cave wall and the giant crab was crushed between metal and rock. The lifeless legs fell away from the window as the drone approached from directly ahead. The image on the small screen slowly came into focus. It was disconcerting as they were seeing their own vessel from the front, hurtling toward the small drone.

"Oh no," Jones said when he could see where the other two crabs were along the hull of the ship.

The interior lights flickered and they started slowing down.

"We're losing power, sir," Marya said. "Redirecting from non-essential systems."

The Hariwulf lurched forward, but it was short-lived. Perhaps drawn by the heat, the two remaining spider crabs had started attacking the engine ports.

"Take remote control of the drone, Marya," the captain said. "We need to peel these monsters off our hull."

"What?" Tom said, pulling his eyes off the screen and looking at Jones. "I thought that tech wasn't enabled."

The crew ignored him.

"Aye," Marya said.

As the drone sped up, rushing toward the Hariwulf, the research sub grew larger and larger on the screen. Similarly, the round body of the enormous spider crab quickly became huge in the viewfinder. And then, suddenly, blam, the drone plowed right into the monster, exploding it off the port wing of the vessel.

"Nice," Ellis said, looking up from his own screen. He and Goldberg were still firing in small bursts, but they couldn't tell if they were being actively pursued down the tunnel. It was almost like the spider crabs didn't want them to go any deeper into the cavern than they had already ventured.

Marya, still controlling the second drone, slowed it down and turned to reverse course. As it powered up and came near the Hariwulf again, they could see that the beast on the port wing was gone, but the beast on the starboard wing continued ripping and rending the metal plates protecting the engine on that side of the vessel. They could see the monster rear back with both huge forward arms and crash them into the exposed section at the same time. The starboard engine shorted out and completely shut down.

Marya sped up the drone and smashed at full power directly into the remaining spider crab. The crew were treated to an explosion and resulting waterfall of blood and gore off the front of the vessel.

Inside the Hariwulf, emergency lighting clicked on.

"Entering the Ice Chimney," Cashlin called.

They had reached the outer edge of the cavern and floated into the middle of the vertical pipe. Marya turned off the picture-in-picture and reset the drone to autopilot with its original flanking commands.

"Hariwulf to control," Jones said. "Come in control."

There was silence from the ship's overhead speakers as well as their comms earpieces.

"Hariwulf to control. Come in control." Jones paused for a few moments. He had pulled the ship around in an about-face to stare back down into the cavern. Ellis and Goldberg had reset their monitors and were ready with the cavitating rounds and torpedoes. Nothing came at them. "Take us up," he said, relinquishing control of the vessel to Marya.

"Aye, sir," she said, leaning forward and immediately plugging a return course into the computer.

**

Marek was reading a data analysis like he was redlining and grading a masters thesis. He had been at it for the last half hour after coming back down the elevator to Section 4. Now, however, a commotion got his attention.

He stood up from his desk and spun on his heels to look around the large room of desks and office cubicles.

Jason. The rookie.

He had come through the main hall into the larger research room showered, shaved and wearing clean clothes. Marek turned the full way around and started walking toward the rookie. Jason, now fully into the room, was doing a little dance and spun one of the female researchers around before dipping her with a cackle. She was laughing the entire time, and the other researchers broke out into a short applause.

"Jason," Marek called, halfway between his desk and the rookie's. At the sound of his name, Jason spun, still laughing and looked at Marek.

"Hey, boss." Jason gave him a salute and kept moving toward his desk. Marek met him there.

"What the hell are you doing? Are you screwing with me right now?" Marek was so mad that it was making physical changes to his body. He was breathing hard as if he had run across the room. His face and neck were flushed in anger. The muscles of his shoulders and arms were tensed in some ancient, rudimentary fight response.

For his part, Jason just smiled. He pulled out his chair, sat down and flipped the main computer on. His three monitors popped live in sequence.

"Are you okay, boss?"

"You're shitting me," Marek said, raising his voice even though he was only four feet away from the young researcher. "You were … not a half hour ago," he stopped and started and then stopped again. "You're late."

Jason stood up and leaned in close to Marek, his lips right next to the elder man's left ear.

"Kiss my ass, Jonah."

And then he turned away, smiling even wider, and sat back down to start his workday.

CHAPTER FOUR
THE RETURN

"SWEET BABY JESUS," she muttered and took a hesitant step backward. The young lady was one of a dozen workers crowded up next to the huge panoramic windows that ringed the Puck. At that moment, even more workers left their desks and jogged to the big window facing East.

They could see a trail of bubbles first, and then the Hariwulf came fully into view.

"Oh, wow."

The hull hadn't been punctured, but the sub was in rough shape. The bubbles seemed to come from either a reserve supply or feeder pipes that had been severed. The vessel was also trailing dark liquid from below. It was hard to tell exactly what the liquid was – it could have been oil, hydraulic fluid or some other engine lubricant – but the fact that it was outside the ship rather than inside was concerning.

Worst, though, was the battered condition of the big sub. There were cuts, scrapes and gashes across the hull. Many centered around the exhaust ports. In fact, there was an enormous severed leg trapped against the body of the Hariwulf. It looked to be about a third the total length of the ship and was trailing a dark, viscous liquid – likely the creature's blood – from the wound.

"Dear God."

The ship was covered in bumps and bruises, but the cargo was in worse condition. The car-sized drone ship was scraped, dented and covered in the same sticky blood that trickled from the appendage stuck in the side of the Hariwulf. Worse than that, though, was the fact that the drone had sustained heavy damage. Parts were missing. There were a couple punctures. It looked like it had been fired upon with artillery shells.

It had only taken forty-five seconds for the ship to gracefully slide upward past the Puck and then out of view. For a few moments, all that was left was the trail of slimy liquid that pooled, swirled and disappeared beneath the sub. During that time, though, nearly the entirety of the research floor had stood and come to the window to look. Even the stoic Jonah Marek stood from his desk for a better look at the catastrophe. He was somewhat invested in the outcome of the mission as the drone itself was a product of his team's partnership with DARPA. He was heartbroken – as much as he was capable – when the first drone was destroyed and sunk to the bottom of the sinkhole only a few days ago. Now, under the protection of the heavily-armed Hariwulf, yet another drone looked to be lost.

"Nice work, guys," he said, rolling his eyes, and sat back down. He had a stack of papers on his desk and noticed, quite by accident, that Jason Rookie was the only researcher who remained at his desk during the show.

**

The launch deck was a flurry of activity as the Hariwulf was hauled aboard. One team extracted the drone to a large, motorized flatbed. They quietly drove it off to be examined and, hopefully, repaired. Another team – a group of scientists from Section 4 – were busy extracting the huge foreleg of the spider crab from the hull of the sub while their counterparts were swabbing what they could of other organic remnants from both the Hariwulf and the drone. Blood, goop and gore were all gently removed from the vessels, tagged with a location and either placed in vials or clear vinyl bags for further analysis. They made a comprehensive circuit of both vessels and then hurried off to get back to their respective labs. It was hard to miss the smiles and overall looks of elation through their protective faceplates.

A third team, joined at first by Jones, walked a careful circuit of the Hariwulf as it was suspended just more than a foot off the floor of the launch deck – held in place by a huge hydraulic lift similar to what might be used in a motor vehicle repair shop.

All the workers, save for Jones, carried a clipboard and were making notes of all the damage. At various points, workers would tuck the clipboard into the crook of their arms and snap off several pictures of some sort of damage. Additionally, some workers would make marks on the ship's hull with a wax pencil to note something concerning. The entire deck was filled with a sort of nervous energy. A strange combination of the heady exhilaration of scientific discovery and the very real notion that they all might die on this expedition.

**

"Something had bothered me about that image," Tom said. They were sitting in the same conference room he had been in just hours after first arriving at Epsilon Complex. This time it was Tom, Jones and the rest of the crew of the Hariwulf. They would soon be joined by Kelly Green, the facility's operations manager, who would run the mission debriefing. They hadn't been allowed a change of clothes yet, so the room stank of sweat and anxiety.

Jones looked at Tom after he said this. The latter was looking down at his notepad where he had started writing his thoughts about the mission.

"What image?" Marya asked. They were lined up three to each of the front two tables. Marya, Jones and Tom. And in the back: Cashlin, Goldberg and Ellis. They were passing the time waiting for the rest of the party – Green, and, likely, some of the section heads.

Tom leaned back and turned sideways so he was facing the other five people in the room.

"When I first saw the image taken from the, uh, the …"

"Galbreath."

Tom snapped his fingers.

"Thank you, Marya. Yes. The image from the Galbreath. The beast that had attacked it and took it to the bottom of the sinkhole. It had appeared on just a few frames of blurry footage. In my mind, at the time, I likened it to a cross between a shark and an eel. Both grown to enormous size. But my subconscious kept chipping away at it."

He paused for a couple seconds, a natural showman, but he also wanted to see if anyone else chimed in with their own thoughts. It had been on everyone's mind during the mission – the huge underwater monster – but no one brought it up. Maybe, collectively, they believed that it would be akin to speaking evil into reality.

"Charybdis," Tom finally said after a moment.

Half those in attendance pursed their brows in thought while the other half widened their eyes in surprise. They had all seen the images in the briefing packet.

"Greek mythology," Marya said. It was half a question and half a statement. Tom simply nodded in response.

"The Strait of Messina, between Sicily and Calabria, posed two dangers to sailors right across from each other. Near Sicily, there was a huge rock shoal – deadly sharp. On the opposite side, was a whirlpool big enough to swallow a ship. To avoid one hazard was to put yourself too close to the other. The two were fictionalized and anthropomorphized as Scylla for the former and Charybdis as the latter. Charybdis has always been illustrated as a huge eel-like monster with a giant, round mouth filled with horrifying teeth. You see, it was the mouth that formed the whirlpool. Resting just beneath the surface and threatening to swallow any ship that came too close."

"It was largely the origination of the idea of being stuck between two equally horrible options. What we generally refer to as being trapped between a rock and a hard place. Either way, you're going to get hurt." Jones was smiling. "Another idiom for the same concept is a favorite of mine: Between the devil and the deep blue sea."

They were all quiet for a moment. Tom rubbed the sweat remnants up off his forehead and into his hair.

"In any event," he continued. "The characterization of the whirlpool monster reminded me of the images of the beast that the Galbreath returned to the control room. I know it's a spurious connection. A whirlpool is a whirlpool. Dangerous, sure, but certainly not a monster. But those illustrations were just too close to be a coincidence. File it away as interesting. Probably nothing."

"Nothing is everything," Ellis said. "But everything is something."

Just then the conference door opened.

"There goes the neighborhood," Jones said, under his breath.

**

Kelly Green entered the conference room with two additional people in tow. They all made polite introductions, but the assumption was that individuals would be preceded by either reputation or station. Standing at the front of the group, the other two section heads took seats in the second row.

"Jonah Marek is with his team on the Puck analyzing the biological samples you have provided," Kelly said. "Including the huge spider crab leg. Cami Ochoa is poring over the data that was burst transmitted and streamed during your mission. She has data sets from both the Hariwulf and the drone. Well, both drones until ..." and she trailed off.

The team was joined by Archer Cavenaugh from comms and David Fontaine from research.

Kelly pulled a rolling desk chair from the corner of the room to the front. She pulled a small digital recorder out of her jeans pocket, activated it and put it on the front table.

"Standard post-mission debriefing," she said, sitting down on the task chair. "We're going over the data from the transmissions as well as the sub black boxes. I just want to hear firsthand from the crew what happened." She paused, smiled and nodded to Jones. "Captain?"

**

All told, the debriefing lasted close to an hour. There were a few interruptions from Kelly and the two section heads to clear up any data inconsistencies or confusion in the order of certain events, but the process ran smoothly. Tom, like the operations manager, took notes of his own while contributing to the information whenever possible. He was thinking ahead to his own personal mission report. The file was already getting quite thick.

After the meeting was adjourned, nearly everyone went their separate ways. Fontaine, though, walked with Tom around the curve of the deck to the crew's quarters. They, ultimately, were at opposite ends of the same corridor. For some reason, Tom had assumed that section heads would have elite living quarters. Maybe Fontaine didn't rank high enough.

"Do you regret going?"

Tom looked at him without breaking stride. He shook his head.

"Not even a little bit," he said. "I suppose it could have all ended in tragedy, but you get a sense of the anxiety and danger when you're down there. I mean, as opposed to watching it on video." He paused for a moment. "I actually wanted to get a sense of the crew. Their training. How they handled pressure. I think I have my answer, though." He grinned and brushed his sweat-dried hair back behind his ear. "I'm not sure I'll be going back down. But, never say never, right?"

Fontaine laughed.

"I don't blame you in the least," he said. "Between you and me, I think this should conclude our exploration. We're a private company, for God's sake. We're not equipped to deal with this level of sea monster. Cryptid. Whatever. Let the military go down there and see what's going on."

"Probably not a bad idea, Fontaine," Tom said, nodding. "Now that they've lost two drones, a manned sub and the level of damage another manned sub took … you gotta wonder how much money the military is ready to throw down the Ice Chimney through you. I'm sure they have some sort of heavily-armed sub they can send to the bottom of this thing."

It was Fontaine's turn to nod.

"I'm sure Kelly's having that conversation with them right now." He paused in front of one particular door in the corridor. "Okay. This is you. Shower, rest, have lunch. Whatever. I know the crew of the Hariwulf is going to meet up on the launch deck to get a better sense of the necessary repairs. To see if the sub is reparable or if it just became a fifty-million-dollar paperweight."

"Sounds good," Tom said, nodding and delivering a mock salute to the section head before opening the door to his cabin.

"Well, this is a fucking disaster," he said to the room and dropped the heavy stack of papers onto the small coffee table before stripping naked and dialing up a boiling-hot shower.

**

It took Tom just a bit more than an hour to scrub up in the shower stall in the far corner of his room and then sheaf through his growing stack of papers. Many were already separated into manilla folders by topic – drone missions, lost drone (1), lost drone (2), Galbreath final mission, Hariwulf final mission, and so on. The most recent two folders had little more than Tom's own hurried notes as they were still waiting for official reports from the engineers, mechanics, researchers and analysts. He put everything in order and read through everything yet again cover to cover. He was taking notes on a legal pad and highlighted certain portions of the reports … questions he had and items he wanted to examine further.

As he finished reading through a folder, he closed it and stacked the next one on top. Soon, it was a pile of folders and a legal pad with several pages filled in with writing, page references and diagrams.

He sat back on the couch for a moment, rubbed his eyes with the palms of both hands and then rubbed the muscles around his temples to try to release some of the tension there. It had just started to work when his watch chimed. Tom hefted an eyebrow and looked at the face of his smartwatch.

He leaned forward back to the coffee table and activated his laptop. He lifted it up and rested it atop the stack of manilla folders. As the laptop fired up, Tom saw several apps open on their own, the last two were a secure VPN and an encryption program. Both asked for two-factor authentication, which Tom provided. After everything had loaded up, he opened a final app – a small communication text box that looked like it belonged more in 1998 than on a modern machine. It was a simple interface, but it was secure and that was all that mattered right now. If anyone happened to be hacked into his laptop right now, they would only see gibberish and the occasional emoticon.

Day two report, came the text prompt on his small message window.

Tom took a moment to collect his thoughts. There was a character limit that he could send at once – giving the encryption program room to work. Finally, he typed a succinct recap of the morning's adventure.

Hariwulf damaged. Lost another drone. Took damage from a host of giant spider crabs. Forty or more. Will visit data analysis next.

He sent that message and then started typing a second, shorter one.

Full extent of damage to Hariwulf unknown. Repairs ongoing.

He took a sip from his bottle of water and waited for a reply or a question. Tom was certain that it would be the latter. Finally, a reply slowly began to materialize out of the encryption program.

Visual confirmation of Alpha?

Negative. Will examine data from mission, but no sighting, sir. He looked at that message for a moment and backspaced over the final word. Sir. Deleted. Tom thought it was a good idea to maintain as much anonymity and, therefore, deniability as possible.

OK. Effects of the Deep Zone probes?

Tom typed: *Nothing concrete. Strong possibility. Will keep digging.*

OK.

And then the message program shut itself off.

**

Tom Granville essentially did as Fontaine had suggested. Shower. Rest. Lunch. The consultant found his way to the company cafeteria and ate at a small two-person table next to the windows. He chowed down while gazing across the waves and the immenseness of the Antarctic Ocean. In the middle distance, he saw what could have been a small pod of orcas – but the color looked wrong. What should have been black and white coloring was a light brown, almost yellow, hue. He shrugged it off remembering that someone on the Hariwulf had mentioned something about the coloring. Was it Cashlin? He couldn't remember, shrugged to himself again, and finished his chicken salad sandwich.

**

The launch deck was awash in activity. Not quite as much excitement as when the Hariwulf had first returned, but there were still teams rushing to and fro. Tom saw Jones standing with a cluster of mechanics and engineers at the stern of the damaged sub.

"I don't know," he heard one man say. "Might take a couple days. Might take a couple hours. We're not going to know until we get panels K, F, JJ and X2 off. The real damage could be under there. Everything else really can be fixed with what we have in the storage closet. Standard operating procedure."

"SOP," Jones said. "Great. Thanks, Jim. I'll let you get to it. Split your team. One works the list from the worst down and the other works the list from the easiest up. Hopefully you can meet in the middle."

"Copy that, Jones."

Jones turned and saw Tom walking across the deck toward him. He spat on the floor and then brushed his boot over the mark.

"Tommy, my boy, you look rested and relaxed," he said, smiling. "Smell a tad better, too. As, I'm sure, I do, as well."

Tom finished walking to the captain and extended his right hand. Jones shook it and turned back to the Hariwulf. He waved his hand in a grand gesture.

"All told, not too bad. Quite a bit of this stuff is cosmetic. Although, some of it got nasty. Those little buggers certainly had it in for us."

Tom stepped closer to the ship and looked at one of the rips in the hull. It was impressive how cleanly the giant spider crab's claws had torn through the metal of the outer shell. That said, he leaned in even closer and saw that the tip of the claw had broken off in the deep gash. He caught Jones's eye and pointed it out.

"Willie," Jones called. "Bring an evidence bag. Got somethin' else for you."

A young man hurried over with a toolbox and went to work gently prying the claw loose before dropping it into a Ziplock bag. He hurried away toward the elevators that ultimately connected Epsilon Complex with the Puck.

"There's a good lad," Jones said, watching the young man hurry away. He turned back to Tom. "A few cables and tubes cut. Nothing essential, but we're going to get it fixed right up and dive back in. A few conduits need to be replaced. The engineers are worried about deeper damage so they're going to remove a handful of panels and look into the ship's guts. Nothing punctured the shielded inner-hull, though, or we woulda been goners."

Tom turned to walk toward the front of the ship.

"One engine should be replaced," he said to the trailing Tom. "I found this interesting."

He stepped around the front of the Hariwulf to the vicious shark's mouth that was painted across the front.

There was a section of the image, though, that looked melted away. Tom, once again, leaned in close.

"Is this paint or vinyl stickers?" he asked the captain.

"Thermoplastic paint," Jones said. "Sort of like the stuff they use on roads. It does a good job withstanding the elements. Snow. Rain. Cars. This time, however, we seem to have lost the battle."

Tom got as close as he could without actually touching it. There were faint traces of some goop around the nose of the craft.

"Is this blood? Do crabs bleed?"

"Sure," Jones said. "It's blue because of the hemocyanin, but they have blood. I'm pretty sure that's what we're looking at. Marek's boys took a bunch off the hull of the sub. This was the only part that actually had paint … seems like the blood chewed through it pretty good."

"Sure did," Tom said and paused, smiling. "It's strange. There's a part of my brain that really wants to touch that goop. To see how it feels. To see if it hurts. The majority of my brain knows to *not* do that, but there's that tiny voice that is chanting do it do it do it do it. It's scary and hilarious at the same time."

"Something like the call of the void," Jones said. He had stopped moving around the sub and leaned against the front port side, just below the big windows. He crossed his arms. "It's a weird phenomenon that humans sometimes get. Standing on a ledge. Standing on a cliff. Standing on the edge of a giant, damn sinkhole in the middle of the ocean. The little voice in the back of our heads keeps repeating one word over and over again." He leveled his gaze at Tom and smiled. "Jump."

The two men were silent. The space was filled with the clatter of workers, chatter, tools and metal-on-metal crime. One man wheeled a huge tool trolley up to the front of the Hariwulf and locked it into place. The man selected a tool and walked away from the men. Tom took a step to his left and leaned his hip against the trolley – crossing his arms as Jones did.

"Did you ever wonder about the origin of the ice cream sundae?"

Tom just looked at him without speaking for a moment.

"What is it with you?" he finally responded.

Jones shrugged.

"I like food trivia," Jones said. "We can talk about baseball or impressionist paintings. Lee Hazlewood. The Grand Theft Auto video game series."

"I'm okay, thanks."

"So, in the late 1800s, early 1900s, ice cream sodas were incredibly popular," Jones continued, grinning. "Couple scoops of ice cream in a tall glass with soda water mixed in. They had crafted something like seventy different soda flavors. Apple, cherry, raspberry, orange. Stuff like that. It was crazy. The big one that remains to this day is the root beer float. Yum." He paused for a moment. Tom stood leaning against the huge rolling tool trolley. There was a big clunk sound from the aft of the sub as one of the enormous, damaged panels was pulled off the hull. Jones didn't flinch.

"Around that time," Jones continued, "some states passed laws forbidding the sale of soda on Sundays. Apparently, the item was considered a sinful vice. Instead of losing all that money, soda fountain owners came up with a great plan. Add another scoop of ice cream to the tall glass and coat it with tasty treats. Chocolate syrup. Whipped cream. Chopped nuts. A cherry. It was no longer an ice cream soda, but an ice cream sundae."

Tom nodded his head.

"Okay."

"They messed with the spelling. D-A-E instead of D-A-Y," Jones pulled himself away from the ship and started walking to the exit. Tom, likewise, moved away from the tool trolley and followed. "Could have been something about copyright infringement. Could have been deferential treatment – you could still buy this awesome treat on Sunday, but we'll change the spelling out of respect."

"Great story, Jones," Tom said, smiling.

"Thanks, bubba. Join me in data analysis?"

CHAPTER FIVE
ANTICIPATED DAMAGE

SECTION ONE. Data Analysis and Digital Storage. It was a huge chunk out of the second floor of Epsilon Complex. The room was sleek and modern with low lighting and about a dozen workstations with banks of huge monitors. Just about a quarter of the room was sectioned off for servers. Even through the reinforced acrylic shielding, Tom could hear the rumble of the massive fans keeping the room cool ... and the hiss of the cleaners venting hot air into the frigid Antarctic afternoon.

There were a group of chairs arranged in a semi-circle around what looked to be Cami's workstation. As the section lead, she garnered the biggest single area in the small cubicle farm. Tom and Kelly sat down and were joined by the rest of the crew from the Hariwulf.

What was left of it, anyway.

"Ahem," Cami cleared her throat, walking across the floor space to her desk. She wasn't trying to get anyone's attention; it was simply a nervous tick. "Here is your backup. The main stuff, we'll be looking at on the monitors."

She walked around the area handing out small, blue binders. They had the Allied Genetics logo emblazoned on the front in gold. The three-ring binders were only about an inch thick with what felt like 100 pages pressed inside. Tom found it odd that there were seven people in attendance outside of Cami – but she had printed out ten copies of the mission report. She put the extra three copies on a corner of her desk and sat down, deftly spinning in her chair so her back was to the workstation, and she faced the group as they started taking their seats.

"Sorry about the folding chairs," Cami said with a half-smile. "I didn't have time to wheel over a bunch of seats from the conference room. Nearest one is the floor above us."

Kelly, for her part, simply smiled and nodded that she should continue. Cami nodded back.

"So, you have the printout of a bunch of stuff. Transcripts of the communication from Hariwulf to control. Internal communication. Mission logs. Depth analysis." She paused for a moment. "I did put a few image printouts in there, but you're going to see the actual feed in just a couple minutes. It's just included for your reference."

She turned her back to the group but slid her chair over so they could see the huge monitor in the center of her command console. There was one big 30" screen with three 23" screens floating above and flanking it. The three upper screens were arranged in a curve. Right now, all four screens showed the same thing: two windows that could not be more different. One was a simple black screen with a command prompt politely blinking. The other was a graphical user interface (GUI) menu system. There were a few folders lined up in there.

"Alright, here we go," Cami said as she hovered her mouse cursor over the first folder in the lineup and double-clicked.

**

"I won't bore you with the play-by-play," she said. "You literally have that in front of you. I've interspersed the mission logs with the transcript … so you can see your position and ambient signals that match what was going on when you were calling in. I've highlighted a few moments, though, that you might find interesting."

The monitors had morphed. The main center console was truly the command console. She had arranged the various files she wanted to access and opened a long, vertical notepad and slid it to the right of the screen. The upper central monitor was divided into a few columns displaying the critical mission data. Things like mission duration, depth, water temperature and status checks of the two drones slid quickly past. The right screen was playing the video feed as it came in from the front of the Hariwulf. As the ship descended, the ambient light got darker and darker punctuated by the strong searchlights attached to the bow of the sub. The top of the screen had the white text HARIWULF (BOW) across the image. The left screen was divided into two and looked similar to the right screen. It was the dual video feeds of the two drones. The top of the left half was labeled DRONE A. The top of the right half was labeled DRONE B.

"We'll pause here," Cami said and hit a button on her keyboard. All four screens froze in place. Tom looked across the three upper screens. There was nothing on the video signal that would cause an alert.

He did notice a number highlighted in red in one of the center screen's data columns. "For about fifty feet, you pass through a warmer pocket of water."

"How much warmer?" Jones asked.

"It fluctuates a little bit, but this pocket of water is about twenty degrees warmer than the water above and below. There must be a horizontal thermal vent. I went back through the historic mission data and can't find anything on visual."

"Was the temperature disagree there in the historical data?" Marya asked.

Cami hefted an eyebrow.

"No," she said. "This is a recent event."

"Great," Jones said.

"Moving on," Cami said and clicked the space bar on her keyboard once more.

**

Cami let the footage and report proceed at a slightly faster rate. She chatted with the mission team while reading through her notes at the same time. She pulled a bright green Post-it note from a page on her report and looked back to the screen. As she stuck the note to the surface of the desk, Tom could see that it was just a string of numbers. When she paused the playback, he realized it was a time code on the video – indicating where she wanted to stop the movie she had created.

"Event number two," she announced to the small room. At the workstations around her, work continued unabated. When they had first started their meeting, the group garnered the occasional glance from the other data scientists. Now that they were about ten minutes into Cami's presentation, the other workers in Section 1 were, frankly, bored. Many of them were the ones who had actually investigated the mission data. The entire team had more than a small pile of work to get through.

On the right-most monitor, the team could see the three subs at the mouth of the huge horizontal cavern.

"Twelve thousand feet," Cami said. "The original kill depth, right? Here, you proceed into the cavern with one drone, leaving the other to act as sentry, right?"

"That's right," Jones said, leaning back in his chair, arms crossed, three-ring binder on the floor between his feet. "I'm not a fan of surprises."

Cami nodded and grinned.

"Yep. Same. You paused for a moment at the crash site of the original drone and then moved deeper and deeper into the cavern. You can see that the temperature is rising again. Not to the degree that we saw in the Ice Chimney, but a significant degree. What you missed is right here, though."

She clicked a few buttons on her command console and all three monitors on top changed. It became a wide panoramic shot of the bow camera of the Hariwulf. Once the resolution caught up to the expanded image, she hit the space bar again, forcing the video forward. It ran quietly for about ten seconds and she paused it.

"Did you see it?"

Everyone sat forward. Jones uncrossed his arms and put his hands on his thighs, leaning forward toward the big series of monitors.

"Yeah," Cashlin said from the far left. "Run that back. But slower."

"Actually," Cami said, smiling. "The best way to see it is to speed it up. Watch." She hit a few keys, and the image began rocking back and forth – ten seconds forward, ten seconds in reverse – at about two times the normal speed. "See?" she said after the sequence had run five or six times.

The entire floor of the cavern seemed to be moving – waving in the undulation of the water as the big sub pushed forward. Cami was back facing fully forward at her desk. The image had been paused and she was typing and manipulating the image with her on-screen cursor. She highlighted a portion of the screen and zoomed in. Once the resolution cleaned up, the entire team could see that it was a floor of –

"Octopi," said Jones.

Cami nodded.

"Giant Antarctic Octopus. Megaleledone Setebos. Not huge. They're only about ninety centimeters from the tip of one arm to one opposite. Just about three feet. These might be slightly above average. Certainly nothing like the spider crabs you faced. The issue, here, is the sheer number of them. I couldn't get an accurate count, but based on the size of the *moving* floor, there could be several hundred."

"We never saw them," Marya said. Her eyes were almost cast downward as if ashamed.

"None of us saw them," Jones said, reacting to her mood. "The ship's sensors didn't pick them up." He turned back to Cami. "Is that why the water temperature went up? All the biology right there?"

"Could be," Cami said. She turned back to her workstation and the three upper screens snapped back to normal. They ran forward as originally set up. She let the footage run forward for about a minute before speaking again.

"My team is working on identifying some interesting attack patterns while coming up with some countermeasures for the hyper-aggressive spider crabs.

Whether we decide to continue deeper into the cavern or further down into the sinkhole, we might come up against them as well. We can't tell right now if they were acting territorial or simply being opportunistic predators."

The footage continued rolling forward. The Hariwulf had now opened fire on the mass of crabs enveloping the big drone. Cami turned her chair to look at the group of people – back and forth from Jones to Tom.

"What I thought was interesting, was this."

She had cued up the command and had only to press the Enter key to run it. Once again, all three upper monitors switched to be the same thing. Instead of one image spread out over three monitors, this was simply the same digital video feed running on all three outputs. The team could see that it was the footage from Drone A. The one they had left at the entrance to the cave as a sentry. It was in the Ice Chimney, facing into the cavern. The camera, though, was the belly cam. It took a moment for the team to figure out exactly what they were looking at but when they saw it, they all gasped.

They were looking straight down into the sinkhole beneath the horizontal cavern. They could see maybe 100 feet due to the strength of the searchlights mounted along the hull of the vessel. They could see, right at the edge of the light, a huge shape sliding effortlessly through the icy depths.

"Charybdis," Tom said, thinking back to their earlier conversation.

As before, it looked like a cross between a shark and an eel. They could see a series of pectoral fins running along the body of the creature, in diminishing size from front to back. There were at least eight dorsal fins.

"It's enormous," Marya said.

The monster took another few slow laps around the walls of the chimney before twisting effortlessly and diving deeper into the sinkhole. At the same time, the drone powered forward – on a collision-course with the Hariwulf.

"Unbelievable," Jones said. "It was waiting for us and got bored."

"Maybe," Cami said. "We're trying to …"

But she was interrupted by ear-splitting warning klaxons and red flashing strobes in nearly every corner of the room. Epsilon Complex was under attack.

Kelly pulled out her phone and opened some sort of status communication app.

"It's Section 4," she said. "I'm heading down." She stood up and pressed a few more buttons to answer the communication and then put the phone back in her pocket. The rest of the meeting attendees stood up as well.

"I'm going with you," Tom said. He noticed Cami pulling out her phone as well. It's possible that all the section heads had the same app. He hadn't really noticed anyone else before.

Kelly looked at him. "The hell you are. Stay up here. Get to your quarters and stay secure. I'll let you know what's going on and when it's safe to reconvene."

She looked at him for a moment longer and then turned to walk away. Tom grabbed her gently by the side of the elbow. He stepped in a little closer.

"I'm coming with you," he said, quietly, away from the crew of the Hariwulf. "If I can help in any way … I **need** to help."

There was something in his eyes that gave her pause. She remembered the demons he was battling and realized that this was just another piece of the puzzle for him – psychologically. Kelly cocked an eyebrow.

"Stay out of my way," she said with a grin. "And don't cause any trouble."

**

The Puck.

As the workers on Section 4 were clamoring toward the express elevators upward to the big complex, a select few people were ready to go down. Tom, Kelly and a handful of security personnel were on a mission to see what was happening below. They were hearing snippets of different conversations as a group exited the elevator and the small group got on.

"Swarm behavior."

"Stuck to the glass."

"Some sort of blue goop."

"Will we get paid for today?"

"Looked right at me."

Tom looked at Kelly and she just shrugged. They got on the big express elevator and a security guard pressed the button for Section 4, entered his access code, and watched the black steel doors slowly slide shut with a hiss. It only took them moments to descend into the depths to the second facility. Epsilon Prime.

In the Puck, they rounded a final corner to find themselves in the main research area. This was the same section of the structure that the group had watched the dramatic ascension of the Hariwulf only hours before. The big room, already reduced to mood lighting, was now a horror story. In addition to the warning klaxons, there were flashing red strobes affixed to every corner of the room, drilled into the ceiling.

"Dear God," Kelly said.

The huge observation windows were covered with a dozen or more octopi. Stretched out, they had a diameter three feet across the widest part of their misshapen star. Tom could hear a gentle thump every twenty or so seconds when a new octopus hit the window and stuck to it, splayed out. They recognized them from the presentation in Cami's office: they were the same creatures that created the organic floor of the horizontal cavern in the side of the chimney.

"That's something you don't see every day," Tom said. He looked around the room and realized that it wasn't totally vacated. The head of Section 4, Jonah Marek, stood off to the right side, right up against the window. He seemed to be examining one octopus in particular. Kelly followed Tom's gaze and saw the man.

"Jonah," she said, striding toward him. "You need to evacuate until we can determine how safe the area is."

Jonah shook his head but didn't turn to face the operations manager.

"Thank you for the suggestion, but I'll be staying right here." He leaned in even closer, his face mere inches from the glass. The octopus seemed to wriggle and pulse a bit. It was hard to say if it was flexing its arms or waving in the current. "It's hypnotic."

Thump.

Thump.

The sounds were coming quicker, now. Tom was trying to think about how many octopi were in the cavern. Seemed like a lot. Could they have all come up to Epsilon Prime? The security team were making their rounds of the Puck and Tom joined Kelly next to Marek.

"What are they doing?" Tom asked the researcher. "Is this behavior normal?"

Marek shook his head.

"Not even a little bit," he said, and turned to Tom as if seeing him for the first time. "Does this *seem* normal to you?"

Thump. Thump. Thump.

What little light had been coming in through the big windows – from the diffused sunlight above and external floodlights – was slowly being enveloped by the mass of writhing tentacles. Marek took a step backward and looked at the wider panorama.

"They're not doing any damage," Kelly almost said to herself. "Are they attacking?" she asked and then trailed off into thought. "Or trying to get away from something else?"

Just then they saw a pod of killer whales glide past just distant from the Puck. They had the same brown-yellow hue that Tom had noticed during his meal earlier. They couldn't tell just how many there were, but they looked huge. Menacing.

"Orcas?" Jonah asked himself, stretching up on his tiptoes to better see through a small window of uncovered space on the display.

The security guards had finished their sweep and walked toward the small group.

"Ma'am, the floor is clear. We should head back to the surface."

Kelly nodded.

"Thanks, Zeke," she said and turned back to Tom. "Gentlemen, if you'll follow me to the tubes."

Thump. But this was worse. BOOM. Something had smashed against the tempered window directly in front of the group. Several of the octopi stuck to the glass simply exploded in a blue mist. The central portion of the window was covered in a blue goop that slowly rolled down the surface.

The group had flinched backward.

"What the hell was that?" Tom asked. But then it happened again.

BOOM.

The window rattled and they could actually feel the Puck sway backward just a bit. There were stabilizing rotors – not as big as the surface complex – positioned around the circumference of Section 4 to reduce sway and keep everything in a locked position. The engines corrected the sway fast enough, but not before the team felt it.

"Ma'am," Zeke said, grabbing the back of her left arm at the elbow. "Really. We should go."

Enough of the splattered octopi had dripped off the window that they had a blurry view of what was happening in the ocean beyond them. Tom gasped. They could see the big orca maybe 100 feet away, blood streaming from its head, turning a wide circle and lining up directly opposite them. It closed the distance in a heartbeat and smashed headfirst into the same window it had apparently hit before. Tom saw a small crack appear in the center of the glass a millisecond before a huge titanium plate slammed down covering the entire window and locking into place.

"Okay," Marek said, his eyes wide. "We're leaving."

**

"It's sort of a blast door," Kelly said after they were back up in the main complex. She, Tom and Marek had convened in the operations center and were watching monitors that played out around the Puck. They had watched the playback from a camera on the top edge of the structure. That last strike had either killed the orca or knocked it unconscious. It floated away from the facility out of the camera's range. It looked like two other killer whales tried the same maneuver against different windows. Suddenly, as if they had heard some signal, all activity stopped, and the pod disappeared. Additionally, the octopi started peeling off the exterior and descending into the darkness.

"All the windows are outfitted with them," she continued. "Any sort of crack or imperfection – and the blast gate slams down in about a quarter of a second. It's designed to protect hull integrity. Clearly, the orca had damaged the window to a point where the shield became necessary."

"Nice," Tom said.

Marek, bored with the display screens, walked over to a communications officer who punched a few buttons on her console and handed the section head a microphone.

"All Section 4 researchers," he said, looking at Kelly. "Breaktime's over. Back to work."

He handed the microphone back without a look and stalked out of the room.

"What a tool," Tom said. Again, Kelly just shrugged.

**

Tom told Kelly that he would meet her in the Puck as they were just starting to examine the remnants of the giant spider crab legs and blood the excursion brought back. He wanted to first swing through the dive deck and check on the Hariwulf's repairs and the condition of the August – the facility's other sub outfitted with the offensive array of weaponry.

He was not alone as both Jones and Marya were in the dry dock as well.

Repair workers had moved the husk of the damaged ship to a corner section of the floor and were busy at work on it. Oddly enough, the vessel looked like it was in worse condition than earlier as the crew had pulled numerous panels off the hull … the panels that couldn't be directly repaired and needed to be replaced. The damage that could be directly repaired was being hammered and welded back into shape.

"That's new," Tom said, stepping up to Captain Jones. The pilot of the vessel turned to look at Tom, who simply lifted his chin to indicate what he was looking at.

Spikes.

"They had added one to reinforce a joint with some extra metal," Marya said, walking over to the two men. "It was kinda small and a little jagged. They were going to sand it down to make it more aerodynamic."

"They ran it past the engineers," Jones cut in, "and found that there wouldn't be a significant increase in drag, so they added them all around."

"To look more imposing?" Tom asked. "Or as a defensive measure?"

Marya shrugged.

"Six of one," she said and smiled. "They sure do look imposing, though."

Tom looked at the Hariwulf for a moment, thoughtfully.

"How's the August? She'll be operational?"

Jones nodded and lifted his chin to the opposite corner of the dive deck. It was a vessel identical –

minus the spiked fins – to the Hariwulf. The August was the other sub outfitted with any sort of weaponry. Kelly was working on a plan of attack for the middle of the night tonight – assuming the sea creatures were somehow diurnal. The three failed attacks had come during the daytime hours. Entering the Ice Chimney at two in the morning might give them some sort of advantage.

"Yep," Marya said. "She's ready. Going through the ops checklist right now. The crew will go through another pre-dive checklist later." She nodded. "We'll be ready."

"Lovely," Tom said.

**

They had congregated near the big windows that covered the side of the Puck where most of Marek's work was completed. The blast shield was still down over the broken section of glass. There were two maintenance workers on ladders working their way around the perimeter of the shield spraying some sort of polymer as an extra sealant. Tom noticed two other members of the maintenance crew making their way around the deck examining each of the other big windows to ensure there was no damage.

Kelly was still in Section 2 working through something with Archer. Tom and Marek were joined by David Fontaine.

"Anything interesting?" Fontaine asked Marek.

"Nah. Giant spider crab that ate a billion-dollar sub. Just another Tuesday."

Marek huffed and turned on his heel to his right and strode off. Fontaine looked at Tom and just shrugged. It seemed to be the only response many people had to

Marek. The two men followed him past the maintenance workers – one of whom was snickering – off the main deck into the big research lab.

Once again, there were three researchers manning the main lab sections. They were all dressed in heavy protective clothing, face shields, gloves and leather aprons. The young man at the table furthest from the door turned and looked at Marek when he entered. He visibly rolled his eyes and turned back to work. Marek's face turned red, but he didn't break stride.

"Good evening, sir," the young lady working at the first table on the left turned and nodded to her boss. Marek waved her off.

The three tables were covered in different specimens. The young lady was working through several vials of the mildly caustic blood and gore that had eaten the thermoplastic paint off the nose cone of the Hariwulf. The second young man had strips of meat laid out along his table. He also turned, smiled and waved to the three men who had entered.

Jason was the rookie researcher on the team but based on his experience and education, he had quickly ascended to a position of authority. He was tasked with the complete arm that had been extracted from the hull of the ship. He was just about to cut into the hard exterior and do a full-on examination of the specimen.

"Any results of note, yet?" Marek asked the room in general. Jason continued to work but the other two researchers turned. It was the woman who spoke first.

"Nothing to report, yet, Mr. Marek," she said. "I'm right now running a chemical and spectrographic analysis of these samples. Was just getting started on a DNA spread to identify and isolate the corrosive element."

Without responding, Jonah turned his head to look at the young man with the meat strips on his exam table.

"Um, same, sir," the man said. "I sent a sample to metallurgy because I was getting some strange readings. Just about to start an autopsy on this piece right here."

Marek stepped forward waiting for the third man to speak but he continued working silently at the end of the room. There was the tiny whir of a small circular autopsy saw as he cut through the tough shell.

"Rookie? What do you have?"

He spoke without turning: "Nothing yet, Jonah. I'll let you know."

Marek's face turned another, deeper shade of red, but he didn't outwardly react. He simply spun on his heel and left the room. Tom looked at Fontaine and lifted an eyebrow in a questioning manner. Fontaine, again, just shrugged.

CHAPTER SIX
ATTACK IN THE BRINY DEPTHS

TWO IN THE MORNING came quickly and painfully. Some operational members of the team were able to take a sleep aid with their dinner and fall asleep at a generally abnormal time. A few tried to nap. A few just gave up and went the other direction. They downed coffee, soda and sugary treats. They played video games, watched action movies or cranked the volume on energetic music. Standing in a line, though, it was almost impossible to tell who had taken which path.

From experience, Tom knew that adrenaline would kick in and hit them all equally like a nine-pound hammer.

The dive deck was, as usual, awash with activity. The August sat gleaming on the north diving platform. The crew of that ship was currently standing around, looking this way and that, completing their own checklists. They had already launched the three companion drones which were just hovering a short distance from Epsilon Complex. The repaired Hariwulf sat opposite the August, looking a little lumpy and weird compared to her sister.

"Amazing," Tom said to Jones as they walked toward the vessel.

Jones nodded.

"Aye," he said. "Maintenance crew double-timed it to get her seaworthy. Kelly gave them ultimate latitude regarding overtime, extra manpower, whatever. They were given the "cannibal" order. They had free reign to strip apart any ship on the platform – minus the August – to use the parts they needed to finish the task. Replacement port propulsion from the St. Cloud. Replacement ballast tanks from the Hemmingway." He paused for a moment. "You get the picture."

Tom nodded in response.

Jones walked Tom over to the August to introduce him to the crew. The crew of the Hariwulf, likewise, was going through the pre-dive lists. More serious, though, because they were examining parts of the hull with the deck's engineers.

"Mr. Gregory, here, is the pilot of this hunk of metal," Jones said with zero preamble. "Young Thomas Granville is the complex's consultant on this disaster of a mission."

Mr. Gregory turned and smiled at Jones, stuck his right hand out to Tom.

"Good ta meet ya," he said.

He was a smallish man of below-average height and weight. He had a shaved head and a thick brown beard that had two patches of gray on the sides of his chin. Tom put his age at mid-fifties.

"My pleasure," Tom said, shaking the skipper's hand.

Mr. Gregory turned and started pointing out the remaining four members of his crew.

"Ben will serve as my co-pilot." He was an enormous man, tall and thick through the chest and shoulders. Late twenties, with hands the size of dinner plates. Tom thought he looked like he would be more at home in a professional wrestling ring or a strongman contest somewhere. Tom nodded to him.

"Our navigator and communications will be Monica." She was a petite girl in her early thirties. Latina. She turned and smiled shyly at Tom. She waved and went back to her checklist.

"Gunners will be Sticks and K-Dom." Two men. One youngish, one oldish. One white, one black. They high fived each other upon introduction and went back to checking the torpedo mounts underneath the vessel.

Tom smiled and gave everyone a casual salute before turning back to the Hariwulf. Jones, though, leaned in and gave Mr. Gregory a hug, clapping him on the back.

"Stay safe down there, brother," Jones said.

"You too, my man."

**

In another corner of the dive deck, the crew of the Hariwulf was ready to go. Joining the pilot, Jones, was Marya, Cashlin, Ellis and Goldberg. Tom, once again, was going along. There was a brief argument with the dive master, but Jones ended it by clapping Tom on the shoulder with a gruff "He's me good luck charm" in his best pirate voice. He leaned in close and added "You can go ahead and call Ms. Green to let her know you put the kibosh on the golden boy's plan, here."

The five team members loaded into the vessel and got strapped into their usual chairs. Tom watched as Ellis fired up the weapons routines. He had minimized the sonar screen and made the targeting array the biggest part of the monitor. He slotted the control interface into place and saw Tom watching him. He pointed to parts of the joystick.

"Trigger is the machinegun," Ellis said, smiling. "Thumb left is small torpedoes; thumb right is the big boy. Just like playing a video game."

He winked at Tom who smiled in return and checked the tightness of his harness.

**

Between them, the five vessels – Hariwulf, August and three companion drones – spat more than four dozen beams of light into the inky darkness of the Ice Chimney. It was already dark, but in the middle of the night, it was impossible to see outside the slivers of light produced by the high-powered halogens.

"Passing 10,000," Marya said.

There was an open comms channel between Epsilon Complex and the two subs: Hariwulf and August.

"Acknowledged," came the response from the comms room two miles above them.

"Kill depth," Tom whispered to himself, remembering the file for the original Galbreath disaster.

"Horizontal shaft approaching soon," Marya continued. "Bearing 232."

"Copy that," came the voice from her equal on the other sub. "Bearing 232."

The convoy, representing almost a billion dollars of military tech, continued dropping further into the black abyss. The sinkhole was shockingly void of life in the middle of the night. They had assumed they'd be joined by nocturnal schools of fish or various deep-sea monsters that were attracted to their light, heat or the vibrations they were putting into the crisp Antarctic depths. However, there was nothing … until…

Clang.

Warning klaxons erupted all over the Hariwulf. Marya was about to announce it over the comms when her counterpart spoke from the August.

"We have movement about 500 feet below us," Ben said. "Seems to be circling. Laterally."

"Full stop," Jones called. Both ships ground to a halt and hovered in the center of the giant hole in the ocean. The three AI drones halted as well. They moved into a triangle formation around the two bigger vessels. "Weapons ready. We wait until the tango is in range."

As soon as he finished that thought, the night became chaos.

"Target on the move," Marya called out. "It's heading straight up toward us."

"Weapons free," Jones screamed in the small sub. Ellis and Goldberg had already activated their control surfaces and targeting screens. Both men were dripping sweat even in the controlled environment. Ellis licked his lips. Jones cleared his throat – a nervous tic.

The monster erupted out of the darkness at them like a giant serpent in a bad horror movie.

Their resulting maneuvers were part of the pre-arranged strategy. The two subs each dropped two depth charges. After only a few seconds there were four muffled WHUMPs that came up from the depth charge explosions. The three drones moved out in a flanking formation. Since they didn't have any offensive weaponry, the drones were essentially sitting ducks. They were only there to provide additional scans and a distraction, if necessary.

All four gunners had pointed their supercavitating cannons directly down. They weren't very accurate but fired magnetic rounds that were nearly the size of those in a jet fighter's Gatling gun. Not all, but some of the rounds found their marks – directly into the body of the sea monster.

It shouldn't have been possible, but they all heard a rumbling scream in their earpieces. Clearly, they had injured the beast. And, more than likely, angered it.

"Keep firing," Cashlin called, her face mere inches from the belly cam of the Hariwulf. The monster was just on the outside of camera and spotlight range. She was waiting for it to appear live on her screens. "Ready light torpedoes."

Goldberg and Ellis responded at the same time: "Aye" and "Copy."

Still firing in three-round bursts, the two men flipped a red toggle switch on the side of the joystick. A new reticule appeared on their targeting screens. It was a bright yellow – almost like a highlighter – that differentiated it from the red machinegun reticule. Ellis lined up a shot with the shadowy image of the SONAR picture of the monster.

"Firing one," he said and pressed a button on top of the joystick with his thumb.

"Firing one," Goldberg said immediately after. Both lightweight torpedoes – a slight misnomer as the weapon was more than 500 pounds and measured six feet long – launched out from the ship and spun around to begin a nearly straight down descent. There was no organic lock on the creature, so the torpedoes were fired to a spot much like an NFL quarterback throwing a timing pattern pass. Unfortunately, the monster saw or sensed them coming and slid suddenly and quickly to its left. The two torpedoes rocketed past it, causing zero damage.

"God damn it," Jones yelled. "Can we correct that firing solution? Go back to rounds." He turned to Cashlin. "Range to target?"

"It's here," she said, all the color draining from her face.

"Evasive action," Marya called to the crews of both vessels.

It was an immediate reaction – the two subs went full thrusters to opposite sides of the chimney. They stayed relatively flat but separated by nearly 100 feet. The drones also shifted position away from the huge monster that was fast approaching. The sea monster, for its part, rocketed upward directly between the Hariwulf and the August. Leaning forward, Tom could see the length and the gaping mouth of the beast. It dwarfed the sub; he shuddered.

"Swivel and unload that clip," Jones called to the crew. Simultaneously, the two subs turned on their axes and aimed at the monster. To his credit, the captain of the August elevated about twenty feet so the two ships weren't directly across from each other. This maneuver complete, both subs opened fire with their cavitating rounds. The August hit with numerous rounds opening puncture wounds along the side of the beast. It felt impossible, but the two crews heard another roar of pain and anger.

The three drones separated with one above the action, one below the action and one generally level with the two subs. They were sending a continuous live video feed back to the operations room on Epsilon Complex.

"Teams, get out of there," Kelly called into her mic.

"Negative," Jones said. "We got this."

The monster looped around, almost skirting the perimeter of the Ice Chimney. It was lining up to get back into the fray. In fact, it was lining up directly at the Hariwulf.

"Oh shit," Jones said. "Prepare full flood port."

"Aye," Marya said.

They heard a second roar and could see the blood trailing after the monster as it got closer and closer.

"Hold," Jones said, silently doing the math in his head. The diameter of the mouth versus the width of the sub. "Now."

Marya had entered a complex combination of commands into her console and hit what Tom figured was something like an Execute or Enter key. Suddenly, the sub dipped to the right and the port thrusters immediately fired on full. The Hariwulf bent down and slid to the right out of the path of the onrushing monster. As it passed them, they were truly able to get a sense of its size and musculature. They could literally see the compression and expansion of the beast's muscles as it slid past. Realizing its mistake, it quickly turned to the right and attempted to line up another pass. Fortunately, the August was ready.

"Fire," Mr. Gregory called. Three torpedoes blasted out from under the August – one heavyweight and two lightweight. The smaller rockets struck first about two-thirds of the way down the monster's body. The impact opened a large wound in its body and the crew heard yet a third roar – this one of pure pain and anguish. The beast whipped around and launched toward the August. The heavyweight torpedo, having never locked onto the fast-moving biologic, rocketed past and exploded against the canyon's wall. The enormous explosion knocked the Hariwulf for a loop. It spun on both axes at the same time as it took several seconds for the automatic hover engines to take over and level the sub. During this tumble, Goldberg struck his head on the command console and immediately fell unconscious.

Tom jumped from his seat and pulled the man to safety – lifting and locking him into the now-vacated chair. Tom secured himself in the gunner seat and looked at the controls to understand what things controlled what. He looked over at Ellis who gave him a wide-eyed and pale-faced nod as if to say *You got this*.

Marya pulled the ship back into position and pointed it directly at the August.

"Oh no," she said.

They were positioned laterally to the action and had a side view of the monster quickly approaching the August. Mouth open. Trailing a stream of gore. The August, for her part, was retreating, but was running out of space.

Tom and Ellis began firing their magnetic rounds. They were technically still within range, but their accuracy was going to be terrible. They both naturally aimed away from the August. Numerous shots raked along the body of the beast … but it did not slow or react in any way. It was on an unwavering collision course with the vessel.

"Brace for impact," Ben screamed into the comms.

There was only a moment of peace before they heard Mr. Gregory shout his final command.

"Fire everything," the crew heard across the comms as the August truly unloaded. They fired their remaining torpedoes and began shooting cavitating rounds directly into the monster's mouth. It didn't matter.

CHOMP.

The beast caught up to and bit down on the August just as the torpedoes struck. There was an enormous explosion in the monster's mouth that engulfed its head and shredded the sub. The sea monster's huge body began to sink, lifeless, into the abyss of the Ice Chimney.

The Hariwulf was suddenly flanked by the three drones as Jones took a deep breath and wiped the sweat from his forehead on the back of his right hand. He cleared his throat.

"Hariwulf to Epsilon," he said calmly. "I have good news and bad news."

**

They landed back at Epsilon Complex just in time to walk into some more chaos. Tom knew there was some sort of issue because of the lack of certain people milling about the Welcome Back party. All the workers from the dive deck and dozens of workers from the big complex in general were there. They were either welcoming back the members of the Hariwulf crew or mourning the loss of friends on the August crew … or both.

The sub's crew had all exited and were shaking hands and waving to those around them. A team of deck workers came over to the vessel to pull it into its parking place to give it a thorough review before giving it the okay for another mission. Through the throng of people, Tom noticed David Fontaine working his way to the team.

"You think it was the alpha?" Cashlin asked the crew, but Jones in particular. "I mean, worst case scenario, there's a city of those things down there. We just happened to run up against their advance scout."

"Jesus, don't even speak that into the universe," Ellis said. He looked over toward his friend Goldberg who was being attended-to by two members of the medical staff. They had sat him down on a folding chair and seemed to be administering some sort of concussion test.

Jones paused and stopped walking just long enough to turn back and look at Cashlin. He stood, hands in pockets, with a lopsided grin but a heavy seriousness in his eyes.

"You know," he said. "The concept of the alpha – stemming from alpha wolf – is a misnomer. Pseudoscience much like left brain-right brain discussions."

He was met with silence, as he usually was. Even Tom was too tired to make a snarky comment.

"People think that wolf packs are led by a vicious dictatorial beast who was either the smartest, strongest, biggest or most savage member of the group. It's a myth. The concept stems from a study that focused on wolves in captivity. You see, wolves in nature are more like a family. The breeding male, the breeding female and their offspring from the past few years. Usually too young to strike out on their own. The pack could be as large as ten wolves, but there is no battle for supremacy. There is a natural pecking order similar to your family. Father, mother, children. It is a natural hierarchy not a royal rumble.

"The study looked at a group of ten wolves in captivity – a Swiss zoo. Even though the author stated unequivocally that wolves in captivity behave much differently than those in the wild, there was an effort by the populace to generalize these behaviors. It's simply not true. Wolves have jobs, that's true. One might be a better hunter. One might be a better fighter. But they are not arranged like that in the pecking order. They are arranged much like a family."

The Section 3 boss reached them at this moment, and they all turned to look at what Tom was looking at. It was just before four in the morning, and Fontaine looked as clean and pressed as he would walking into the office after his wake-me-up coffee. His eyes were bright and the only thing marring a beautifully pressed button-down shirt were the visible sweat stains under both arms.

"Well, *that's* not good," Tom said under his breath.

Fontaine made his way to the five crew members and shook the captain's hand.

"Glad to see you back in one piece, Jones. Thank you for your aid in ridding us of that menace."

Jones shook his hand and nodded his thanks. You could see the pain flash across his face. They destroyed the sea monster, but at what cost?

With the Hariwulf safely on the dive deck, Tom heard a huge clunk as the first drone was hauled out of the water and carted back to a holding station. Receiving no response from Jones, Fontaine continued.

"Try to get some rest," he said. "Debriefing at ten-hundred." Everyone nodded and began to walk away. It was unlikely they would be able to get back to sleep after the harrowing adventure 10,000 feet beneath the wave swells of the Antarctic Ocean, but they could at least grab an early breakfast and relax in their private quarters. For Tom, however, Fontaine caught his arm as he walked past. "We've got a problem."

**

"What's up, Fontaine?" Tom asked once they were clear of the rest of the crew. "Where are the rest of the section heads?"

Tom had pulled up even with Fontaine. They turned a corner into a completely empty corridor. Epsilon Complex seemed to be a strange mix of quiet areas with celebratory gatherings. It was probably best summed up by Jones thirty minutes or so ago – good news and bad news. Two sides of the same coin. Two versions of the same event. They had defeated the monster but had lost yet another submersible – and its crew. Five individuals, now dead. Probably only half the facility knew what had happened. The rest had been fast asleep ready to take over their first shift duties.

"We're trying to keep it low-key for now," Fontaine said, rounding another corner and coming to a bank of elevators. "Jonah Marek is missing." The elevator door slid open, and Tom and Fontaine stepped into the huge area – all by themselves.

**

It was a skeleton crew on the Puck, running experiments, tabulating data, cleaning. The night shift. Tom didn't recognize any of them from either his time on Section 4 or the larger complex in general. He and Fontaine received a few questioning looks, but no one outright approached them. It must have been strange to see section heads down here at this time of night.

"What do you mean *missing*?" Tom said. "This is a closed facility. Not like he went out for pizza."

"Exactly why everyone's a little freaked out. There was a short meeting called right after your launch and he never showed. We've been asking around. Looking for him. Since then. Kelly's trying to track security footage while we're going floor to floor. It was time to hit the Puck and Kelly wanted me to grab you off the dive deck. I mean, this is a closed environment. The perfect example of a closed environment. It's not like he went out to grab a burger and fries."

He paused for a moment, looking around the large observation deck. The blast shield was still down across the cracked window.

"But here we are," Fontaine said.

They had made their way halfway around the area, checking all the offices and closets along the path. They found some interesting little cot rooms where workers could get a quick catnap during a long shift. They found the huge walk-in freezer where they stored specimens. They found Marek's trophy room with numerous specimens and replicas from past victories. But no Marek.

They had made it to the tech area of the Puck, with a few big servers and three monstrous workstations – ones that mirrored Cami's from above them. Hand on the door handle, Fontaine stopped.

"What?" Tom asked.

Two seconds later, the warning klaxons went off yet again.

"Section 4, brace for impact," came a voice over the loudspeaker.

"Terrific," Fontaine said. He took his hand off the handle and the two men ran back to the big observation area.

"Evacuate Section 4," called the voice from Epsilon Complex's control center high above.

The small handful of people working had immediately jumped up and ran for the four express elevators that would whisk passengers through the twenty stories of frigid ocean water between Epsilon Prime and Epsilon Complex. When the researchers had all evacuated, Fontaine and Tom got into an elevator. Just then, they felt an impact on the west side of the structure. Due to the flexibility of the anchor cables, the Puck swayed about six feet to the left and then swung back like a pendulum. As Tom's elevator doors closed, he could hear the loud THUNK as another blast shield slid down into place. Whatever had hit the structure had damaged one of the windows – in one hit compared to the many required by the psychotic killer whale the previous day.

"Lovely," Fontaine said, wiping the sweat from his face with the sleeve of his left arm, further marring his once-pristine button-down shirt.

**

They made it to the main complex with only one more shuddering impact. Tom and Fontaine could feel the vibrations travel all the way up the elevator cable. It was so disruptive that it actually caused the passenger capsule to slow noticeably and the emergency systems struggled to figure out how to respond.

There was an aide waiting for them when they stepped off.

"Ms. Green is waiting for you in operations."

"Thanks, Rose," Fontaine said and cocked his head sideways to indicate to Tom where they needed to go.

Operations was chaos. But, somehow controlled. It was a testament to Kelly Green's ability to run a team through a disaster – and her experience with past troubles. There was a huge monitor surrounded by banks of smaller monitors. On the big monitor, Tom could see a top-down view of the Puck. He thought it must be embedded in the central support tether due to the clarity and proximity of the image. There might have been some digital trickery as well because the image was unmarred by what should have been the presence of the support. It was being removed in real time – much like the human brain simply erasing the sight of one's nose out of the visual field.

Tom smiled, thinking that would be the kind of trivia that Jones would share in an inappropriate moment. His smile, however, faded seconds later as he could see what was causing all the trouble.

"Oh my God," he said, gasping at the image.

It was another sea monster.

"That's not the same," Kelly started, turning to Tom. Captain Jones had just entered the operations center as well.

Tom shook his head.

"Nope," Jones said. "We blew his damned head off. This is a shiny new nightmare."

Suddenly there was another gasp from the room. Tom and Kelly looked back at the huge monitor. The sea monster had finished its circuit of the circular structure and peeled off in a straight line to the east. It lined up from a distance and sped full force into the building. Section 4 swayed in the impact and one of the elevator cables snapped. They watched in horror as the 200 feet of vinyl/rubber hybrid slowly fell through the water. The Puck listed slightly to the side of the missing support. Not only functional, the four elevator cables all carried a weight load alongside the main central support.

"Jesus," Kelly said. "Reel it in. Get the Puck up here."

One worker jumped up from his station and ran to a special console in the corner of the room. He punched in a long code and had to take a necklace off ... it held a key much like you'd see in a movie about nuclear launch codes. He turned the key on the side of the panel and a thick acrylic door slid open. Behind the door was a huge handle currently in the **down** position. He grasped it and pulled it to the **up** position.

There was a groan as heavy machinery began slowly pulling the big structure up to the underbelly of the main complex. Tom watched the status bar and information that was spilling along one of the monitors on the workstation nearest him. According to the diagram on the side, the Puck would ultimately sit right under Epsilon Complex in its resting position. This was how the entire structure was ferried around the world to different research spots. According to the ticker, it would be a slow process. Suddenly, though, the complex shuddered and all movement stopped. Kelly turned to look at the ops worker who had initiated the transfer.

"We have a problem, ma'am," he said. "It looks like all that movement might have jammed or crimped the mechanism."

Green pinched the bridge of her nose and closed her eyes.

"Send it back down," she said, opening her eyes and looking at the worker. "Take a team to the spindle. Launch a drone. Figure out what the hell is blocking it."

"Aye."

Jones reached forward and tapped Tom on the shoulder. "Fancy another go?"

"Let's try to kill it without blowing ourselves up," Tom replied.

"Solid plan."

The two men ran from the room to get to the dive deck.

**

The mission failed before it even started, though, as the Hariwulf was essentially on blocks in the corner of the deck. Workers had moved to remove the two main rear fans that provided thrust. One had been damaged in the last mission due to the concussive blast of the heavyweight torpedo.

"Oh, you've got to be kidding me," Jones said.

The group of mechanics looked up at him.

"Routine, sir," one of them said. "It was due for replacement anyway … and three fins were bent. It would lead to a catastrophic thrust failure."

Jones closed his eyes in defeat. Tom, though, furrowed his forehead and pursed his eyebrows. He was remembering something from the last mission. The ghost of a memory. He wasn't sure what his subconscious was trying to tell him.

"How long to install the new fans?"

The group of mechanics all looked at each other for a moment. The main one, who had done the talking so far, shrugged and looked up at the skipper.

"Forty-five minutes," he said with another, smaller shrug.

"We'll all be dead in forty-five minutes," Jones said, turning on his heel and jogging back to the operations center with Tom in tow.

On the way, he said: "The August and the Hariwulf were the only operational subs with any sort of offensive weaponry. We have other big vessels, but the best they have is depth charges. They pack a wallop, but not in this kind of fight."

He slowed to a stop and turned to look at Tom.

"Actually," he said. "You head to operations and see if you can help Kelly. I'm going to the below deck to see if I can help those kids trying to unstick the reel."

"Copy that," Tom said. Not sure what else to do, but somehow feeling it was appropriate, he stuck his right hand out. Jones shook it, wheeled, and headed to the flight of stairs in the corner.

**

As soon as he walked into ops, the flurry of activity overwhelmed him. The entire facility now was awake and at their stations. He came in just in time to see another monster impact. The structure groaned. He could see on a digital diagram on a monitor that four out of the eight blast shields were now down. The beast was simply pummeling the Puck. Perhaps he had a difficulty getting to the main structure on the surface. For whatever reason, Section 4 was taking the totality of the damage.

Kelly saw him come in and walked over to him. She leaned in close so only he could hear.

"I'm going to lose the Puck," she said. "My career is over."

Tom looked from her to the big monitor and back.

"Would a Pyrrhic Victory help your case?"

"What do you mean?" she asked.

He shrugged. "Well, if you're going to lose the Puck, what if we figured out a way to take out the monster at the same time?"

She frowned.

"Is there some sort of self-destruct mechanism or something? Something we could set and then blow the structure up with the monster along with it?"

She thought for a moment.

"This isn't Star Trek, Tom," she said, still frowning. "We don't build stuff with the expectation that we're going to eventually blow it up." She got quiet again, thinking about the footage from the August blowing up and taking the beast's head with it. The same image Tom had had earlier. The Pyrrhic Victory – winning the battle but losing something significant in return. Finally, she spoke up again.

"There might be a way to create a feedback loop and overload the generators," she said. "It wouldn't be like a timed explosion, though. We'd have just the same chance of blowing it up with the fish a hundred yards away than we would with it right next to it."

"Is it worth the chance?" Tom asked.

On the big monitor, there was yet another impact. A second elevator cable snapped and the central support groaned with the added weight.

"It might be the only chance," she said. "But it can't happen from up here. The loop would have to be initiated from down there."

Tom laughed and nodded.

"Well *of course* it would," he said. "And why wouldn't it?" He thought for a moment. "I'll go. Tell me what to do and I'll go. I'll zip down, set up the loop, and come right back. Then we can all pray together that the timing works out in our favor."

Kelly thought for a moment.

"I couldn't possibly ask you to do that," she said.

"We're running out of time," he said. "It's my chance to be a hero. If it doesn't work, this way you can lay the blame on me. I'm already tainted goods, remember?"

Kelly was quiet for a count of ten seconds. Twenty.

"Okay," she said. "Take a wireless comm set so I can talk you through it from here." He turned to leave. "And, Tom? Straight down and straight back. No sightseeing. If you have to pee, then just piss your pants. Time is *not* on our side. Those other cables are going to snap much faster with the added load. I need you to force the overcharge and get back here double quick."

"You sure do paint a picture," he said, smiling. He took a step toward the door, stopped, turned back to her. He leaned in and gave her a quick hug. Kelly wasn't sure how to respond, so she patted him on the shoulder blades – almost a brotherly motion.

"You're back here in ten minutes, okay?" she said. "No dawdling."

"You said it, boss."

CHAPTER SEVEN
NEGATIVE SPACE

HE FELT DOOM AND PEACE at the same time. Tom estimated that he had less than a 50/50 shot at getting this done and back up the elevator. Clearly, the sea monster was mad about the loss of its brother or sister or wife or whatever. It had fixated upon the Puck as the object of its rage. Essentially, it was half-destroyed. Two elevator cables had snapped, and half the blast shields were down covering damaged observation windows.

There wasn't much time.

If Jones could get down here with some firepower, that would be something. If Epsilon could send some depth charges, that would be something. Unfortunately, the engines were out of the Hariwulf and they couldn't risk the depth charge explosions with Section 4 hanging on by a thread.

Kelly had agreed to send the remaining fleet of drones down to try and distract the monster so there were none … or at least fewer … impacts while Tom was down there. The drones would be remotely piloted by humans. Apparently, they were able to reprogram or eliminate whatever glitch stood in the way of this functionality.

"Comms check," Tom said as he stepped off one of the two remaining elevators. "I've arrived at the Puck. All is quiet."

"Great," Kelly said in his ear. "Keep moving. You're going to want to get to the electrical room. Back left office in the center block from you. You think you can do that?"

"Sure. It's not like I'm going to have to fight a giant spider or something."

Kelly wasn't sure if he was joking.

"Have you ever had to fight a giant spider?"

Tom shrugged even though no one could see him. "Just the once."

BLAM

As he turned the first corridor, running, he was immediately slammed against the wall to his right. And almost as immediately as he heard the thump from outside the structure, he heard the instant whizz-clunk of yet another blast shield falling into place.

"You okay?" came Kelly's voice into his earpiece.

Tom shook himself, rubbed his shoulder for a moment and swayed with the motion of the Puck. As it had all the previous times, Section 4 swung way out away from the impact and then swung back. Tom steadied himself with a hand on the wall.

"Yeah," he replied to Kelly. "So far, so good."

He reached the maintenance door for the electrical conduits.

"Drones are engaging," Kelly said. "Hopefully we can reduce the amount of impacts you have to absorb for the next five minutes you're down there."

"Copy that," Tom said. "Message delivered. I'm here, by the way. What's the code?"

He reached out to touch the keypad that was on the right side of the door and then stopped, his hand quivering in the air.

"554655," Kelly said.

"Um," Tom said.

"Tom, we don't have time for this."

"Um," he said again. "There's blood on this keypad."

**

Kelly looked around the big operations room. She looked up at the huge central monitor that was showing a static image of the Puck from above. It swayed a little in the remnants of the current left behind by the giant sea beast. It was still being supported by the main central column and the two remaining elevator cables.

She looked across the room at the group of eight people sitting huddled over their glowing laptop screens. The group was a motley collection of pilots and computer techs. They took a quick poll to see who the eight best pilots were on the entire complex … no matter the profession or area of expertise. These were the result. They were piloting the eight remaining drones in and around the proximity of the monster. There was a line of monitors along the north wall of the room that each displayed a view from each drone's nose camera.

"There's *what*, now?" she said.

**

"Yeah," Tom said. "Blood. All over a couple keys." He punched in the code and the light on top of the control panel flashed from a steady, resting red to green. Tom heard the internal locks disengage and he reached forward to grasp the handle.

The door opened inward. Thick cables and black conduits ran circles around the room all over the walls and the ceiling. It was a tight area – a forward corridor with a wall on the left and heavy steel racks supporting cables that snaked their way from the floor to the ceiling. This was the electrical brain of the hovering observation structure. There was a computer monitor and several latches, buttons and toggle switches on a small workstation against the left wall. Twelve feet into the room was a turn to the right. Tom had looked at the schematic before coming down here. The electrical conduits ran through four sets of racks arranged in lines. From the top-down view of the blueprints, it looked like a library.

There was something else.

"I think I found Marek," he said, standing just inside the arc of the door.

Sticking out from the right-hand turn were a pair of sneakers, attached to a khaki-pant-wearing pair of shins. The body was laying on the floor with just the lower portion of the legs visible from Tom's POV.

"Oh, shit," Kelly said. "Great. He can help you."

"Um, he can't help me." Tom looked down to his feet. The cold vinyl tiling that made up the floor. He could see some drops of blood and some smears here and there. "Pretty sure he's dead. Dragged himself, bleeding, into this room and died. He's not moving."

Kelly was silent for a moment. So much death and destruction in the last few days.

"Okay," she said, taking a deep breath – in through her nose, out through her mouth. "Forget him. Do you see the console?"

**

Kelly walked him through the process that would culminate in an explosive feedback loop that should destroy the Puck and the sea monster at the same time. The mechanical room was a bit warm, but Tom was pouring sweat from the stress and the worry that Section 4 would soon fall into the abyss. This always had the potential of being a suicide mission.

"Alright," Kelly said over the comms. "Get out of there. It should take somewhere between five and ten minutes until a failure cascade. You gotta move."

"Copy that."

He turned to leave the room but was interrupted by Kelly's voice in his ear.

"Oh no."

WHAM

It was horrible timing as Tom was right in the middle of the doorway when the devastating impact hit. The jarring motion slammed the side of his head against the metal of the entryway's frame. With a sickening thud, he fell to the floor, not unconscious, but woozy and unsteady on his feet.

"Damn," he said to himself, putting the palm of his hand, gingerly, up to the side of his head. He brought the hand back down, checking his palm for blood. There was none, but a huge knot was already forming at the impact spot. "Ow."

"You okay?"

Tom pulled himself back to his feet and stood in the doorframe: back against one side, arms outstretched to the other side to steady himself. He was about to answer when he heard a horrible metal groan and a metallic snap.

The third elevator cable broke and floated down past the Puck. Tom looked out around the doorframe at one of the few huge acrylic observation stations that remained open. It was pure luck that he could see the cable falling down past the hovering structure. It was waving in slow motion. The research facility listed heavily to the right.

"Get out of there," Kelly screamed into her microphone. Tom's head jerked to the side away from the ear holding the speaker. The entire structure was only being supported by the big central column and the one remaining elevator cable. It was only 40% of the engineering supporting 100% of the weight. The sway of the Puck slowed to a stop, but the list remained.

Tom pushed himself away from the doorjamb and something caught his eye – in his peripheral vision. The lights in the station started flickering – the first symptom of the overcharge. The mechanical room looked like something out of a horror movie. The flickering lights in the small area caused something of a strobe-light effect. Tom saw someone stepping over Jonah Marek's body at the end of the corridor. He was dressed like a strange combination of a surgeon and a researcher. Lab whites, heavy apron, gauntlet-style gloves that traveled all the way up his forearms. Worse, though, was the knife.

And the blood.

"Okay," Tom said to himself. "I didn't expect that."

"What are you doing?" Kelly yelled. "You need to get up here right now."

Tom backed out of the electrical access room without taking his eyes off the blood-covered individual staggering toward him. Through the acrylic mask on his face, Tom could see the man's face. He was foaming at the mouth and had a bizarre wide-eyed look to him. For a moment, Tom thought he recognized the man. Wasn't he a researcher who was working on the crab legs? When was that? Yesterday? Two days ago? The blurriness of his head made it hard to concentrate.

A section of overhead lights exploded and sparks from the now-exposed circuitry rained down on him.

Tom turned to his right and started running down the corridor away from the mechanical room. He could hear some squeaking as the killer's sneakers chirped against the bloody tiles in the room when he gave chase.

"There's, uh, there's a guy with a knife," Tom said.

"Tom, I don't care. You need to get on that elevator right now."

"On my way," Tom said, sprinting around the final corner that put him right in the middle of the research and experimentation cubicle farm. He looked up and out the few windows that were still unblocked by the titanium blast shields. It was almost pitch black outside as the exterior flood lights had long ago flickered off. Tom could see the lights of the drones swirling about like a field of stars. He knew there were eight in total but could only see two right now. The Puck gave another lurch and Tom slid to a stop.

He saw a hazy reflection in the glass and turned to look behind him. The maniac with the knife was running toward him. When Tom turned, the bloodied man began screaming, knife raised to his shoulder height. He was maybe ten steps away when there was an awful crash as the monster split the two drones like a goal post and slammed headfirst into the side of the Section 4 structure. Tom caught a glimpse of the monstrous row of teeth before the big shield crashed down over the window.

The jolt sent Tom to the floor. It also threw the rookie's momentum for a loop as he slid sideways. His head struck the corner of the nearest desk and he fell to the floor – unconscious or dead. Tom didn't wait to find out as he pulled himself upright and sprinted toward the short corridor leading to the elevators.

"Tom," Kelly yelled.

"Heading there now," he said. "Which one is still operational?"

"Southeast," she said. "I've already sent it down. It should be waiting for you right now."

The lights in the Puck suddenly became incredibly bright as too much power was being generated in the small space. Several bulbs and LED panels exploded, showering the area with sparks.

"I'm there," Tom said, reading the big elevator door. He reached forward to punch the call button when the structure groaned around him. With the elevator door open, the final cable snapped, jolting the stability of the facility. The doors, linked to the emergency setting, slammed shut again.

"Oh God," Kelly said.

"Yeah," Tom replied.

**

The emergency lights ran the area's perimeter and cast the Puck in a sickly green glow. In the back of Tom's mind, he realized that they must be activated by the ambient light. Most of the facility's lights had blown out. Tom jogged back to the main office area. The bloody maniac's body was still there, motionless, on the floor by a corner desk. With only the central structure in place, the Puck was gently swaying from side to side. It was like being on a huge cruise ship. Tom could feel the motion, but it wasn't enough to knock him down.

"I've launched the three manned subs," Kelly said in his ear. "Zurich, Hemmingway, St. Cloud. You need to make your way to the escape hatch in the top of the facility. Their ETA is thirty-five seconds. Get a move on."

Tom was silent for a moment.

"What depth was this structure tested to?" he asked, quietly. Slowly.

"With the blast doors down," she answered, voice thickening. "It was tested to 20k."

Tom nodded. They had thought the Ice Chimney might be as deep as thirty-thousand feet, but it hadn't been fully explored. If the Puck fell that far, it might survive long enough to get a rescue operation underway.

Then he remembered that the entire thing might explode in the next three minutes.

"Damn," he said to himself.

"Twenty-five seconds, Tom. Get a move on. There's an access ladder right in the middle of the facility. The subs can dock there and get you out."

"There's no time, Kelly," he said, the structure swaying even heavier, now. "This thing is going to break loose and blow up before those guys can dock." He paused for a moment. "Call them back. I don't want them caught in the wake."

"Tom," Kelly said.

RIIIP

It was a huge groan and rending sound as the final support, the large central column tore clear of the top of the Puck. Suddenly, the big structure began falling into the abyss. Seeing it fall off into nothingness, the sea monster gave chase. Followed closely by the eight drones that kept transmitting their video feed. Maybe it was the shape, maybe it was because it was filled with air, but Section 4 seemed to be falling slower than it should have.

Tom sat down on the floor, cross-legged, facing the single remaining open window of the structure.

"Five thousand," someone said in the Epsilon Complex operations room. Kelly didn't bother to repeat it to Tom.

"It's been a pleasure, Tom," she said instead.

Tom nodded. He smiled.

"Make me look good in the report," he said.

On the main video feed, they watched the sea monster rear back for another attack. Suddenly, out of the darkness, three more sea monsters exploded upward toward the Puck.

"Count on it," Kelly said.

"Ten thousand," came the same voice from control.

"You've got company," she said.

Tom, again, nodded.

"The more the merrier."

The four enormous serpents coiled around the falling object hoping to squeeze the life out of it. The first monster had started biting against the corner of the structure.

Boom.

The drones had slowed but were still sending back video. Much of the entirety of Epsilon facility workers had crammed themselves into ops or stood outside looking in through the windows. Every screen was showing the same image from slightly different perspectives. The Puck, barely visible around the writhing mass of flesh that surrounded it, exploded and took the four remaining sea monsters with it.

The footage was silent, but the image was unmistakable. The Puck had erupted and was engulfed in a cloud of inky gore – the blood and pieces of flesh that remained of the four beasts.

"Shit," Kelly said. "Mark the tape. I gotta call the director."

EPILOGUE
RAW ALIGNMENT

EVEN THOUGH THE BACKGROUND WAS BLURRED, Kelly could tell the man was sitting in a high-rise office. When he moved, the blur effect around his body dispersed and she could see small remnants of a picture window, blue skies and the tops of distant skyscrapers.

"Yes sir," she said, responding to his question. "Totally destroyed. Three dead. Tom, Marek and an unaccounted-for researcher named Jason Cabrera."

"That's a shame," the director said. "Tom performed admirably?"

"Absolutely. He sacrificed himself to end the threat."

"Okay. We'll include that in the report." The director paused. "Did he start digging into the military contract?"

"Not that I know of," Kelly said. "He was focused on the leviathan. Leviathans, in fact."

The director was silent.

"We've collected numerous samples," she continued. "I had sent all the remaining drones for observation, and they were in close enough proximity to swoop in and collect a great deal of … evidence."

The director nodded. He pushed his glasses up the bridge of his narrow nose with the index finger on his right hand.

"Okay," he said. "Okay. We'll send out a replacement for Marek. Start working on the samples as best you can." He thought for a moment. "Take half of what you collected. Vacuum seal it. Pack it in ice and ship it to the facility in Crimea. They're doing some wonderful things with cloning up there. Maybe we can get what we were after in that way."

Kelly Green thought for a moment and then nodded. It looked like this was probably the natural conclusion of Operation Deep Zone anyway. Capturing, cloning and controlling a kaiju. A never-before-seen sea monster. Some sort of cliché movie villain.

"Yes, sir," she said. "Crimea."

"Send me a copy of your report before you finalize it," the director said. "I might have some revisions. Sugar to satisfy the board." He paused for a moment. Kelly simply nodded in response. "And don't lose any more equipment. We're pulling the facility out of there in a month. We'd like to retain as much value as possible."

"That's my goal, sir," she said and smiled before ending the transmission.

THE END

AFTERWORD
GREAT BLUE HOLE

IT'S FUN, AS A WRITER, to try to identify just where a story idea came from. This one is a pretty clear image in my head. The Great Blue Hole off the coast of Belize. I can't remember exactly where, but I remember scrolling through social media about a year ago and seeing the image – Lighthouse Reef surrounded by gorgeous blue-green water with a perfectly circular darker hole right in the center. The image had a boat zooming through the area to give it some size and perspective.

Breathtaking.

As all writers do, I filed it away that there were sinkholes in the ocean. An obvious revelation, but one that I hadn't even considered. I made a note of *great blue hole* in the stenographer's pad I keep on my desk and went back to writing whatever I was writing at the time.

A pile of months later, publisher Red Jack Press was reprinting a sea monster story I wrote called "The Beast of Trash Island" in serial form and I thought, *Hey that was fun to write. I should write another one.* And, thus, I started scanning through the dusty folder of my mind to see if there was anything in there worth exploring.

The Great Blue Hole.

I hope you enjoyed it, kind reader, as it was fun to research and write. It took a little longer than I had anticipated because I was working on other projects (writing that one, editing this one, revising that one … it's all a huge conveyor belt!) but it was nice to usher it across the finish line. It was fun to leave bits and pieces for the readers to fill in, though, rather than spell everything out. Yes. There was more than one horizontal cavern. No. There were no more of that particular monster down there. Yes. The military probes had awakened them. Yes. The Ice Chimney went well past 30,000 feet. And so on.

I don't write many sequels, and I don't think there will be a sequel to this one. Although, to be fair, I'm always intrigued by the idea of the evil version of Microsoft. A giant, global conglomerate that has lost all semblance of compassion and reality. Allied Genetics always seems to fit that role. Maybe they're doing something equally horrific in another part of the world. It wouldn't surprise me.

One other thing, detail-minded readers will realize that this story takes place in my little universe before the dinosaur/time travel/action/science fiction stories I wrote as we learn that Allied Genetics is still in control of the gigantic facility in Crimea … which we later find out to be an abandoned military complex called Objekt 221.

Keep reading; keep writing!
Steve Metcalf

Author Bio

STEVE METCALF has explored writing short fiction, novellas, novels, feature length screenplays and screenplay shorts. Rather than sticking to one path of style or genre, he simply follows his muse and writes whatever inspires him. From a book about the history of the videogame industry to zombies rushing forth from an abandoned Peruvian mine, nothing is off limits.

You can interact with Steve at www.steve-metcalf.com

Also By Steve Metcalf

RESET: A Videogame Anecdote
Sketch
The Beast of Trash Island
Objekt 221
Hell Island
Project: Reaper
Temple of the Spider God
The Merchant of Time
Curse of the Red Pyramid
Lot 23

King Paranormal Investigations Series

Coldwater
Ten Brooks Manor
Paradox Iron

The Event Series

The Event: The Chicago Rust Yards
The Event: Iron Bay
The Event: Precision Robotics
The Event: Gold Rush
The Event: Wreckage
The Event: Congo Square

Check out other great

Sea Monster Novels!

Michael Cole

SCAR

Scar is a killing machine. Born from DNA spliced between the extinct Megalodon and modern day Great White, he has a viciousness that transcends time. His evil is reflected in his eyes, his savagery in his two-inch serrated teeth, his ruthlessness in his trail of death. After escaping captivity, the killer shark travels to the island community Cross Point, where prey is in abundance. With an insatiable appetite, heightened senses, and skin impervious to bullets, Scar kills everything that crosses his path. His reign of terror puts him at war with the island sheriff, Nick Piatt. With the body count rising, Nick vows to protect his island community from the vicious threat. With the aid of a marine biologist, a rookie deputy, and a bad-tempered fisherman, Nick leads a crusade against Scar, as well as the ruthless scientist who created him.

Rick Chesler

HOTEL MEGALODON

An underwater luxury hotel on a gorgeous tropical island is set for an extravagant opening weekend with the world watching. The only thing standing in the way of a first-rate experience for the jet-setting VIPs is an unscrupulous businessman and sixty feet of prehistoric shark. As the underwater complex is besieged by a marauding behemoth, newly minted marine biologist Coco Keahi must face off against the ancient predator as it rises from the deep with a vengeance. Meanwhile, a human monster has decided he would be better off if Coco were one of the creature's victims.

Check out other great

Sea Monster Novels!

Michael Cole

MEGALODON VS COLOSSAL SNAKE

Brought to life by the miracle of DNA cloning, a 93-foot Megalodon shark has escaped captivity. With an insatiable appetite and unmatched aggression, it travels west for the Georgia coast, leaving a path of destruction in its wake. Bullets and harpoons can't penetrate it, steel nets can't hold it, and it's only a matter of time before the whole world finds out about it. In a race to stop the beast, the organization responsible recruit a marine biologist and a herpetologist to develop a plan to catch it. To do it, they must unleash the company's other genetically modified experiment—a 150-foot snake, resurrected from the DNA of the mighty Titanoboa. The pursuit leads to inevitable combat, and the scientists are forced to witness the deadly realities of genetic tampering. As the battle escalates, it is clear nobody is safe...and that nature never intended for these beasts to return. As the destruction mounts, and the death toll climbs, the true loser of Megalodon vs. Colossal Snake is humanity.

Tim Waggoner

TEETH OF THE SEA

They glide through dark waters, sleek and silent as death itself. Ancient predators with only two desires – to feed and reproduce. They've traveled to the resort island of Las Dagas to do both, and the guests make tempting meals. The humans are on land, though, out of reach. But the resort's main feature is an intricate canal system . . . . . . and it's starting to rain.

Check out other great
Sea Monster Novels!

Matt James
SUB-ZERO

The only thing colder than the Antarctic air is the icy chill of death... Off the coast of McMurdo Station, in the frigid waters of the Southern Ocean, a new species of Antarctic octopus is unintentionally discovered. Specialists aboard a state-of-the-art DARPA research vessel aim to apply the animal's "sub-zero venom" to one of their projects: An experimental painkiller designed for soldiers on the front lines. All is going according to plan until the ship is caught in an intense storm. The retrofitted tanker is rocked, and the onboard laboratory is destroyed. Amid the chaos, the lead scientist is infected by a strange virus while conducting the specimen's dissection. The scientist didn't die in the accident. He changed.

Alister Hodge
THE CAVERN

When a sink hole opens up near the Australian outback town of Pintalba, it uncovers a pristine cave system. Sam joins an expedition to explore the subterranean passages as paramedic support, hoping to remain unneeded at base camp. But, when one of the cavers is injured, he must overcome paralysing claustrophobia to dive pitch-black waters and squeeze through the bowels of the earth. Soon he will find there are fates worse than being buried alive, for in the abandoned mines and caves beneath Pintalba, there are ravenous teeth in the dark. As a savage predator targets the group with hideous ferocity, Sam and his friends must fight for their lives if they are ever to see the sun again.